Praise for Six Weeks to Yehidah

Melissa Studdard weaves a dreamscape for her main character Annalise – a true Hero's Journey in the Joseph Campbell sense. The story is delicate and poignant – a far cry from the usual fare for young adults. The theme is universal, the writing is skillful, poetic and memorable.

~**Dr. Ian Prattis** author of *Failsafe* and *Earth My Body, Water My Blood*

Combining the clever word play of Lewis Carroll, the delightfulness of the Oz books, and the philosophical underpinnings of both C.S. Lewis and the Buddhist *Bodhisattva, Six Weeks to Yehidah* is a tour-de-force of excellent writing and startling imagination, and a gentle exploration of the interconnectedness of all things.

***** Five stars.

~**Dave Hoing,** co-author of *Hammon Falls* and *Voices of Arra*

Six Weeks to Yehidah is a spiritual delight, a page-turner fantasy that takes its readers on a journey not to be missed. Melissa Studdard makes a brilliant debut in this young adult novel with memorable characters, powerful scenes, and intimacy rather than spectacle. The story is intelligent and compelling, a must-read for spiritual literature fans of all ages – refreshingly original, haunting, and heartfelt.

~**Adele Kenny**, *Tiferet* Poetry Editor

Six Weeks to Yehidah is the story of Annalise, a young girl who enters a wondrous dreamscape. With the company of two very special friends, she takes a journey and meets a variety of intriguing and highly entertaining characters. Ultimately, it is up to Annalise to solve the greatest riddle of all: why she's here, and what it all means. Her each step toward this answer is both delightful and thought-provoking. *Six Weeks to Yehidah* is a must read for anyone who knows there is more to life than what is right in front of our eyes.

~**Jen Knox**, author of *Musical*

Set in the hyperactive imagination of an adolescent girl, *Six Weeks to Yehidah* is a delightfully palatable study of such timeless issues as Universal Authority. Flanked by her two favorite sheep, Mabel and Mimi, young Annalise roams the fantastical realm of the clouds, encountering self-proclaimed deities. The lush, magical imagery is worthy of *Alice in Wonderland* and *Gulliver's Travels*.

~**Marina Julia Neary**, author of *Brendan Malone: the Last Fenian*

SIX WEEKS TO YEHIDAH

Melissa Studdard

ISBN: 978-0-9846517-0-2

Library of Congress Control Number: 2011935058

Cover art by: KnoxworX multimedia, www.KnoxworX.com

Author photo by: Jennifer Ayers.

Published in 2011 by All Things That Matter Press

Acknowledgments

There are many wonderful people who contributed to this book, and to them I express the utmost gratitude. First I'd like to thank my family. My daughter, Rosalind Williamson, offered both inspiration and astute feedback throughout the entire composition process. She also wrote the poem that Annalise recites in the first chapter. As well, I'd like to say thank you to my parents, John and Lorrie Studdard, whose unconditional love and support have been the force behind almost every good thing that has happened in my life, including this book.

Many friends also played significant roles. Anastasia Voight, Jeanie Bernard, Jen Knox, and Dorothy Wood Wilson offered feedback and moral support, and it was Anastasia who initially sparked the idea that became *Six Weeks to Yehidah*. Sally Sontheimer and Linda Leschak generously read and critiqued so many drafts of the manuscript that they probably lost count. This book would absolutely not be what it is without the insights they provided. As well, Marisa Iozzi Corvisiero, of L Perkins Agency, offered some essential early critiques. For constant moral support, I'd like to thank some of the writers who, with the friends mentioned above, I consider to be part of my ever-expanding writing family: Donna Baier Stein, Adele Kenny, Chuck Taylor, Keith Linwood Stover, Aparna Mudhedkar, Jeremy Birkline, Elizabeth Myles, Dave Hoing, and Udo Hintze.

I'd also like to thank my publishers, Phil and Deb Harris, who have been warm, helpful, and welcoming since the day I signed my contract. Deb's superb editorial skills not only fine-tuned this book; they taught me some lessons for the next time I sit down to write.

I'd like to thank Donna Baier Stein, publisher of *Tiferet Journal*, for running Chapter Seven, "The Portal" in the August 2011 issue. I'd also like to thank Vishwaneth Bite, publisher of *The Criterion*, for running Chapter One, "Hagski's Domain," in his Summer 2011 issue, along with an interview about *Six Weeks to Yehidah* conducted by Aparna Mudhedkar.

Thanks also to Mark Knox for the cover design, trailer, and other creative contributions. And thanks to Ryan Mendenhall, Amanda Fisher, Kylan Voss, Albert Chang, David Lugo, and Taylor Simon, of Otakurai Games for their creation of the interactive *Six Weeks to Yehidah* WEB site.

And, finally, I am eternally grateful to my teachers and to the writers before me, who are far too numerous to name and who inspired me more than I could ever express.

~For Rosalind~

The soul level most connected with the source of awareness is called yehidah, which means unity. It is the center point of the soul and as such it disappears into the infinitude of creation. Some would say that this is the aspect of the soul that is "hard wired" directly into the essence of the Divine. It is not "with" us but we are never apart from it. This is where duality dissolves. It is far too subtle for human consciousness. Yehidah is our ultimate link with God, the part of us that can never be separated from the Divine. When all else fails, the awareness of our yehidah endowment may be sufficient to carry us through our most difficult of times.

~Rabbi David A. Cooper

TABLE OF CONTENTS

CHAPTER ONE
HAGSKI'S DOMAIN

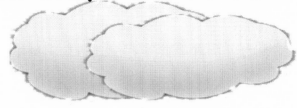

The thing you would notice most was the rain, how the rain fell and fell and never seemed to stop. The sky was constantly swollen with it, then birthing it, swollen, then birthing again, and the hills, like greedy babies, suckled up all that rain. They shone and glistened green as the backs of frogs on bright green lily pads.

In a small village nestled in these hills lived a girl named Annalise. She had just turned ten, which was old enough to begin thinking about grown up things, like choosing her own clothes for school, yet young enough still to indulge in fanciful imaginings of enchanted trees and talking hills. Her best friends were the clouds that canopied her village and the verdant hills that hosted her most precious and outrageous dreams. She would lie on the grass with her hair fanned around her head like a halo, and there she would talk and sing and make up stories all afternoon long, with no audience but the clouds and the sheep to hear her tales. There she would stay, despite the rain, until the very last minute, when her mother called her in to supper.

But this one Friday, when Annalise's school was on vacation and she'd slept in and then eaten an especially late lunch, she decided to try to outlast the rain instead of going inside at dinnertime.

"I'm not hungry," she called back to her mother. "Please just let me stay a little longer."

"Okay, okay," her mother said. After such a late lunch, she wasn't exactly hungry herself. "But stay where I can see you from the kitchen window."

"Thank you, Mom!" Annalise called, moving a little closer to the house so her mother could see her.

Annalise spun around with her arms outstretched and then fell to the ground, laughing and singing.

"I love being outside," she said to Mabel and Mimi, the two sheep who had followed her back to the house.

It began to rain a little harder, and Annalise strengthened her resolve to stay outside no matter what the weather. She was, you could say, as stubborn as the rain itself. And even though she had good intentions regarding her mother's wish that she stay within sight, it wasn't long before she became enchanted with a flash of light off in the distance. Someone with less imagination might merely have assumed the light to be a firefly or a flickering lamp, but to Annalise it was a golden fairy riding a rain drop to a magical kingdom. In fact, it reminded her of a poem she'd written in school earlier that year. It went like this:

> A frigid winter's night
> Leaves on fir trees glistening with snowdrops
> Fairies skip across the night sky
> Joyous in their eternal dance
> The Man in the Moon smiles fondly
> At his children on Mother Earth
> The path reflects the glistening heavens
> A fox passes, unwavering
> Unaware of the sky, the heavens,
> Concerned with the darkness,
> Finding his way

She recited the poem to herself as she watched the flickering light, and soon her mind went the way of her imagination, and she began to create new poems about fairies and rain drops and foxes on trails, and not a thought was left in her head about staying near the house, much less near the open kitchen window.

Annalise chased the flashing light to the base of the hill, all the way down to the river bank where she watched it dance atop the glistening water and skip from pebble to pebble. After landing briefly, the light darted into a cluster of trees, then dashed up through their tops, up into the clouds and back down again, where it skipped from treetop to treetop, twirling in between.

"I've seen this imp before," Annalise said to the sheep who had followed her to the base of the hill. "But now that I'm closer, I don't really think it's a fairy. It must be some other sort of magical being, something even more unique. I'll stay here and figure out just what it is. Then I'll write a story about it."

True to her word, Annalise stayed in the valley between the hills, even after her mother had called her home again, which, being so far away, she did not hear. The rain, stubborn as it was, remained also, and the magical light flickered and danced a merry show for Annalise and the sheep. The river rose, and evening turned into night, and as Annalise remained oblivious to the passing of time, her mother grew concerned and began to look for her, eventually calling the local authorities, who put together a search party.

When by the next morning, the villagers had still not found the little girl who was as obstinate as the rain itself, the floods started to reach the tops of the hills, and the search had to be abandoned so that helicopters and boats could take local families to safety.

Annalise, in the meantime, had fallen asleep right in the midst of singing "Zip-a-dee-doo-dah" and had then awoken to find herself, Mabel, and Mimi transported to the other side of the clouds, the place above where rain is made.

***

It was the brightest waking up she'd had in many Saturdays, so even though she felt some curiosity as to her whereabouts, she decided to christen the morning with a song, "Sunny Saturday," which she made up as she went along.

"I'll figure out where I am in a little while, when I find someone to ask," Annalise thought, and then she began singing her song, which went something like this:

Oh, it's a Sunny Saturday
(baaa)
Sunny Saturday indeed
(bleat)
For here I am
On the other side of the clouds
(baaa)
With my favorite sheep
Mabel and Mimi
(baaa baaa)
Sunny Saturday
Sunny Saturday indeed
Tra La La Li
Tra La La La
Everything is so fluffy and white
(baaa)
Mabel, Mimi, and me
(bleat)

It was a full chorus. Annalise was lead, and the sheep, who could only say "baaa" and "bleat," were back up.

But that all changed in an instant, because Mimi did something unexpected. No sooner had the song ended than she shouted out what she thought to be "bleat," which meant, of course, "lovely job with the song, my dear companions." However, what came out when Mimi opened her mouth was not "bleat" but the *actual words*, "lovely job with the song, my dear companions."

Mabel, Mimi, and Annalise were so surprised that for a moment they all just stared at each other in complete silence. Then Mabel said, "Why, Mimi, you can speak real words."

"And so, it seems, can you," Mimi replied.

The two sheep, who were excited beyond measure, spent the next several minutes trying out new words on each other and practicing pronunciation, while Annalise, whose vivid imagination made her an expert at managing extraordinary happenings, remained unsurprised and busied herself making up real words to replace the "baaas" and "bleats."

"Try this," she said, humming a few bars to the sheep. Then she hummed again, and the sheep hummed with her.

"Now for the words," she said, lifting her arm like a conductor holding a baton, but before she got to the words she was interrupted by the most horrid voice she had ever heard. It seemed to come out of nowhere, and it sounded like a car screeching to a stop in order to keep from hitting a dog.

Annalise, Mabel, and Mimi looked all around, but there was no one in sight.

"Who is that singing in my domain?" the voice demanded.

Annalise jumped backwards, startled by the voice again, as she still could not see a body to go with it. Then, regaining her composure, she replied, "Why, it's just me."

"And who, exactly, is this 'just me' who is bold enough to reply to the divine Hagski?" the voice demanded.

"Me, Annalise," Annalise responded, shuddering. Although she could see this Hagski nowhere, she imagined her exhale as she spoke to be a gassy cloud of black fumes, like the exhaust from an old car.

"Not me and you?"

"No, just my sheep and me, Annalise."

"Annalise of?"

"What?" Annalise said.

"Annalise of the Enchanted Forest, Annalise of the Queendom of Munchkins, Annalise of the Hundred Acre Wood, Annalise of the Shimmering River, Annalise de la Mancha, you know, Annalise *of –*"

"Um, well, Annalise of the Verdant Hills, I guess."

"You guess? Well, what is it, girl? Are you from the Verdant Hills or not? Are you orphaned? Adopted? Exiled? Restricted? Did you trespass? Are you a clone? Is your brother a dung beetle? Did you escape from a firing squad? Were you mortally wounded and then left for dead only to be rescued and given to a king who was not your father but who would rear you as his own until you discovered, mistakenly, that you were destined to kill him and so you ran away, only to end up accidentally killing the man who was actually your father, thereby fulfilling the prophecy?" Hagski paused for effect, then said, "How can you not know which Annalise you are or from whence you hail?"

"Well, I don't know about clones and dung beetles and all that stuff," Annalise replied. "But I am indeed Annalise of the Verdant Hills, and you can tell anyone I said so."

Hagski now appeared before Annalise, and Annalise saw that she was indeed a hag, and quite a frumpy mess besides. Her hair was primarily black, but big chunks had been dyed pink and orange, and one side was matted to her face as if she had just woken up from a sweaty nap. She wore a wrinkled beige button-down shirt that had mud colored stains scattered about it.

"Oh, a feisty one," said the hag. "I like that. Are you a Yahoo or a Houyhnhnm, Easterner or Westerner, male or female, Christian or Buddhist, living or deceased, vegetable or meat?" And with this, she began to poke at Annalise with a chopstick that she pulled out from over her ear.

"Skinny little thing, ain't ya?" she said.

"Stop it!" cried Annalise. "That hurts!"

"Ah, meat it is, then, definitely," said Hagski, pulling out her notebook and jotting something down. "Most who come here are. It's been a long time since the carrot girls were here, or the green bean boys."

Annalise took advantage of the fact that the hag was writing instead of asking questions for the moment, and she began to look around to try to comprehend where she was and what was going on. She figured that if her sheep could now talk, she must be in a land with new rules. Then it dawned on her that she was not really in a "land" at all. She was in the sky, and gravity no longer had the same effect on her. It pulled her, yes, but only to the top of the clouds, which she found surprisingly firm to walk upon.

"Pardon my directness," said Mabel, "but where are we?"

"You are in Hagski's domain," said Hagski. "What comes here stays here. We are a democracy, and I am the dictator. You are my new slaves. Here are your rules:

Rule #1   Always follow the rules
Rule #2   Be prepared to recite the rules upon command
Rule #3   If you break the rules you will be punished
Rule #4   Anyone caught trying to change the rules will be exterminated
Rule #5   No discussing the rules with other slaves
Rule #6   Any misinterpretation, misrepresentation, mispronunciation, misinformation, misjudgment, misunderstanding, misplacement, misconduct, miscounting, miscuing, misfiring, mishandling, misspelling, or misreading concerning the rules will be punishable by law.

"Do you have any questions?"

"Yes, I do," said Mimi, leaning toward Hagski in confusion. "What exactly *are* the rules?"

Hagski looked furious. "You nincompoop," she screeched. "You half-witted, turnip-brained, baaaaing, bleating, comedian wannabe sheep. I just clearly outlined the rules for you, one through six. Follow them!" She paused her diatribe to roll her eyes. Then she asked, "Does anyone have any *real* questions?"

"Yes," said another screeching voice from a nearby cloud. "I have some questions."

Annalise, Mabel and Mimi craned their heads around and even turned their bodies to try to see where the voice was coming from, but there was no one to be seen.

The second voice began its list of questions:

1. Have these rules been approved by the rule approval committee?
2. Do they contradict previous rules, current rules, or rules that are to be made in the future?
3. Have they been revised by the rule revising committee?
4. Have they been edited by the rule editing committee?
5. Were they passed by the rule passing committee?
6. Have they been catalogued and cross-referenced with other rules?
7. Have they been printed on committee-approved paper, with committee-approved ink?
8. Have they been numbered and labeled?
9. Were there rules made to determine how these rules would be evaluated by the evaluation committees?
10. Were subcommittees created to monitor the progress of the primary committees?
11. Was there a committee formed to make sure that all committee members were on the appropriate committees?
12. Is there a meeting planned to address these questions, and if so, has this meeting been approved by the meeting planning committee?

"*Excellent* questions!" said Hagski. "I'm so glad I'm not the only one with a brain around here!"

Soon Hagski and the second sky voice digressed into a verbal skirmish regarding the fine points of a rule which neither of them had yet identified. Annalise thought it sounded like they were arguing about two different rules and that if they identified the rule, maybe they would find that their differences were not so great after all.

"Perhaps you should identify the rule," Annalise said.

"Hogwash," said Hagski.

"Cockamamie," said the other voice.

"We both know we are arguing about Rule #207, 928, Section 72, Addendum A, Revision #39, Amendment Pending Results of Rule #132," said Hagski.

"Actually," said the other voice, "I was talking about Rule #17."

"Well," said Annalise. "The thing to do, clearly, is to first discuss Rule #17, and then, in a separate discussion, talk about Rule #207 and whatever else you called it."

Surprisingly, Hagski and the other sky voice agreed, after which they promptly appointed Annalise as chairperson of the Rules Discussion Committee of the sky, with her sheep, Mabel and Mimi, as her only committee members.

"Hagski," said a new voice from behind a haloed cirrostratus cloud. It was a voice that was bold but kind, and filled with humor. "Are you hazing the new arrivals again?"

"Why, indeed, no," said Hagski. "I'm just having me a bit of fun, a little poking and a little prodding, a little singing and a little songing, a joke here, a whistle there, tilting a windmill every now and then. I'd never slay a sleeping dragon."

Annalise acted quickly upon hearing a kind and sensible voice.

"Hello," she offered.

"Hello back," volleyed the haloed voice.

"To whom am I speaking, please?" she asked. She stood on a thin line of clouds, her two sheep beside her, and Hagski facing her. The cirrostratus from which the kind voice emanated loomed large in the distance, the sun shining behind, around and through it.

"You are speaking to Me," the voice replied, sounding as warm as the sunlight that seemed to be its source.

"Me who?" she asked.

"Me Anyou."

"Pardon?"

"Don't worry about it right now. We need to get you situated. Do you know why you're here?"

"No," said Annalise. "I don't even know *where* I am, much less why."

Hagski shuffled around, looking a little embarrassed. It was not Hagski's Domain after all. Me Anyou was clearly in control, a fact which made Annalise, Mabel, and Mimi feel quite pleased.

CHAPTER TWO

ACOUSTIC ISLAND

Now there appeared before Annalise a translucent, glowing, yellow man. If you could imagine light in human form, that is what Annalise saw.

"Are you Me Anyou?" she asked, tilting her head to the side for a better view of the man.

"Oh, no, no, my dear," the light man replied, chuckling to himself. "I am simply *one manifestation* of Me Anyou, one of billions and trillions and more. You may call me Bob." And with that, Bob turned on his heel, leapt forward, and began to bounce an aerial hopscotch from one cloud to the next. "Follow me," he shouted back over his shoulder.

Annalise followed, Mabel and Mimi trailing behind. They happily left Hagski in the dust.

"Where are we going?" Annalise shouted.

"*There,*" Bob answered, continuing to hop.

"Where is *there*?" Annalise asked.

"Not *here*," Bob said. "At least not yet. But soon it will be!"

"Oh." Annalise's brows pulled together in confusion. "Then when will we be *here*?"

"We're always *here*," Bob said, smiling back over his shoulder at Annalise. "Every time we get *there*, it becomes *here*. That's why it's best not to trouble about it."

"Well, *when* will we arrive?" Annalise asked.

"Not *now*," Bob answered. "At least not yet."

"Because *then* will be *now* when we arrive?"

"Sort of," Bob said.

"So it's best not to trouble about it?" Annalise asked.

"Correct."

"So if we shouldn't worry about *where*, and we shouldn't worry about *when*, what do we do until *then*?"

"That's the part you need to understand." Bob said. "There is no *then*. There's only a chain of *nows*."

"Oh, dear," said Mimi.

"My heavens," said Mabel.

Annalise noticed that the sheep were now walking on their hind legs and standing upright like humans. She started to comment but then thought of a way to get the answer she wanted from Bob and turned back to him.

"Okay, so what do we do *right this minute*?"

"The same as every minute," Bob answered. "Enjoy the trip from now to now. Plant your feet firmly on a cloud. Tell the truth about everything, but sometimes tell it slant. Be kind to all living creatures, even yourself. Close your eyes before you leap. Steer your vehicle with wisdom. Make up a song to commemorate any event, no matter how big or small."

"Oh, that's easy. So I just keep on doing what I already do?"

"Yes, just keep on," Bob replied.

Annalise decided that if she wasn't allowed to worry, then worry she would not. Worse things could happen than not knowing where you were or where you were going or when you would get there. She quit asking questions about when and where. She looked around at the wide blue sky and giggled to see Bob skipping from cloud to cloud. She delighted at the hilarity of cloud hopping with sheep and a Light man, and she even did a little spin and hopped a few clouds backwards. Then, what do you know, as soon as she quit wondering and instead started being, she found that now had finally arrived, for when she leapt to the very next cloud, she landed on something that was the same size as a cloud but was not a cloud at all. It was, instead, a small island, and surrounding it was not air but water.

The sun was already starting to set, and Annalise realized that although it had only felt like minutes, they must have been cloud hopping a long time.

From this island, Annalise leapt to another island and then another and so on until she found herself finally walking on the sandy banks of a larger island. The sight she saw on this island was quite unusual: Clusters of musicians sat in session at the shoreline, each band playing without regard to the others so that absolute pandemonium reigned. It was like when you draw a picture and then color over it with so many different colors that the whole thing just turns an ugly shade of brown. No one would know that under the muddy brown crayon markings once lay a pretty picture, just as no one could tell if any of these bands were making good music under the muddy noise they created when combined.

"Oh, my heavens," Mabel shouted, trying to be heard over the din.

"Dearie me," said Mimi.

"What?" shouted Mabel, holding a hoof up to the side of her mouth and leaning forward.

"I said, 'Dearie me.'"

"I'm glad to know you sheep can still speak here," shouted Annalise.

"Why, yes, indeed," said Mabel. "It sounds as though they may be in need of some good backup singers."

Annalise noticed that maracas and castanets hung from the trees like coconuts, and drums and cymbals littered the beach instead of rocks and shells. Chairs were positioned around pianos, and people picnicked and played cards at them just as if they were tables. Stranger still, a lifeguard sat atop his perch, blowing sunscreen from a tuba onto a crowd of frolicking children below.

More toward the middle of the island, where the grass grew thick and the soil was rich, flutes, oboes, and clarinets rose from the ground like stalks of corn. And further still, in the distance, bells hung from vines like a new, musically endowed version of flowers.

"Take your pick," Bob said, waving his hand toward a crop of woodwinds. "We have everything you've ever heard of, and even some you never have. Look at that baby grand over there. They just harvested her last week. Beautiful. The cream of her crop."

"Are you a genetic engineer?" asked Mimi.

"Is that why we can speak now?" said Mabel.

"And stand up?" said Mimi.

"Did you design us?" they chimed.

"Oh, heavens no," said Bob. "I'm just a guide. I've been with Annalise for a long time. It's just that none of you noticed me before. It's not always easy to see the light."

"Oh, yes. I do remember you now," Annalise shouted. "You were my imaginary friend. I used to carry you around in my left hand, and everyone marveled about how I could tell left and right apart even when I was so young. They couldn't see you in there. Bob. The imaginary friend. You weren't always just light though, were you? You were all kinds of things, like a butterfly or a beetle or even a crisp wind. Where did you go?"

"Only where it was necessary to lead you, Annalise. Mostly to the hills."

"So you were there all along?"

"Yes, I was, starting at a certain point, anyway. But never mind all that now. It's time to pick an instrument and play with the band."

Annalise walked forward, into the woodwinds, and pulled a ripe bassoon off a stalk.

Bob looked troubled.

"Not for you, my dear," he said, gently removing the bassoon from Annalise's hands. Then, indicating Mabel and Mimi with a sweep of his arm, he said, "I meant them."

"But we're just backup singers," Mabel said.

"Yeah," said Mimi. "Our voices are our instruments."

"Well, why didn't you say so?" Bob said, nodding with approval while at the same time handing Annalise a baton. As he did so, Annalise noticed a small, heart-shaped scar in the web of his hand between his thumb and forefinger.

"This is for you," he said to Annalise.

Annalise's eyes widened as she grasped the full import of Bob's gesture.

"You mean I have to conduct this madhouse of musicians, bring order to this chaos?" she whined. "Me? Why me? Why do I have to do it?"

"Because they're waiting, and because it's a lesson you must learn by doing. Here on Acoustic Island, the musicians have lived their entire lives in a state of disharmony. They all have their small circles of family and friends, and the members of each circle just play among themselves, without any regard for the other groups. They are completely unconcerned about the discord they're creating overall. It's like they can't even hear each other."

"Clearly," said Annalise, looking with dismay at the separate groups of musicians on the beach. "But how can it be fixed?"

"It can only be repaired by an outsider, someone who can see the big picture, someone who can champion the aural health of the entire island, someone, Annalise, who can put harmony before their own interests."

"How can that be me?" Annalise asked. "I don't even know what 'aural' means."

She turned to Bob for an answer, but Bob had disappeared.

"Mabel, Mimi," she pleaded, "what should I do?"

"Well, Bob said before that you should keep on," said Mabel.

"That's right," agreed Mimi. "Let's keep on keeping on."
And together they sang:

> Tra la la la,
> tra la la li.

They looked at Annalise to provide the main lyrics, but she just stood and stared at them. They stopped singing.

"What's wrong, Annalise?" asked Mimi. "Don't you love to sing?"

"Yes. I just don't think that's the way to solve the problem this time. We'd only be adding to the noise."

Then, seeing that she'd hurt the sheep's feelings, she added, "I like what you sheep are singing, but you can't sing it alone. We have to get everyone to work together. We have to find harmony, or there's no way we can enjoy our song, and then what's the point of singing?"

Annalise felt exasperated. She plunked down on a drum to think, and when she did, it made a muffled, hollow sound.

"Think, think, think," she said to herself, tapping her temple.

"Wow," said Mabel to Mimi. "Everything is an instrument here. Look, Annalise is even playing her head."

Annalise was oblivious to the sheep's comments, and she continued to tap at her head as if she could thump an idea right out of it.

"It's so loud on this blasted island that I can't even hear myself think," she said.

"Well, then, we'll be quiet," shouted Mimi.

Annalise stopped tapping. "Be quiet? Why yes, that's it," she exclaimed. She jumped to her feet and hugged Mimi, nearly knocking her over. Mimi, you see, was not yet used to standing up and being hugged at the same time.

When Annalise backed up, Mimi could see that her face was lit with the glow of an idea.

"Thank you, you beautiful, talented, perfect specimen of a

sheep," Annalise said.

Mimi looked confused. "I have been quiet many times," she said. "Yet never have I received such praise for it. Why are you so pleased this time, Annalise?"

"You silly, brilliant sheep," Annalise said, backing away a little more to make eye contact. "It's not that *you two* are going to be quiet. It's that you gave me the idea to get *the musicians* to be quiet. When they're quiet, we can communicate with them, and then we can get them to play together. Mimi, you made me realize that silence is the beginning."

"Well, that's right," Mabel said. "We knew that. We just didn't know we knew it."

Annalise started to twirl in circles and sing:

> On a noisy island,
> a noisy, noisy island
> a super noisy island
> indeed,
> with Mabel and Mimi,
> my two favorite sheep,
> on an ear-splitting island,
> a noisy, chaotic island
> a super noisy island
> indeed!

Mabel and Mimi clapped their hooves and whistled with joy. Their spunky Annalise had sprung back to life now that her mind was no longer weighed down by the heaviness of trying to solve a problem. The trio danced up the beach together toward the nearest group of musicians, and, as they danced, sand glittered like fairy dust in their wake.

When they got to the first group of musicians, they stopped to listen. Five mustached musicians, all dressed in pale blue tuxedos, appeared to be warming up for a formal gig. Their black hair was long and slicked back, and they each had a prominent gold tooth with the letter "G" in it. They looked like brothers.

"Pardon me," shouted Annalise. "May I speak with you, please?"

There was no response whatsoever. The musicians ignored her and kept playing as if she weren't there at all.

"I said, 'May I speak to you, please?'" Annalise shouted.

The drummer stood up, and, walking slowly in a large circle, used his drumstick to draw a line around himself and his band.

"This," he said, "is the no cross line. *Don't* cross it."

He resumed playing the drums.

Annalise stood on the outside of the no cross line and shouted, "I agree not to enter your circle if you will speak to me, *please*."

But, again, the musicians ignored her. It was as if the line in the sand enclosed them in a soundproof zone.

"Can we bring you dinner?" Annalise asked, thinking the musicians would have to quit playing at some point in order to eat.

She was wrong.

"We have no need of sustenance," the drummer replied. "Only privacy. Please leave. We have very important work to do."

"I don't understand them at all," Annalise said to Mabel and Mimi. "It's as if they don't get any joy from the music. So why do they do it?"

"Beats me," Mabel said.

"Me, too," said Mimi.

Annalise felt exhausted but not demoralized. She walked off, toward the moonlit field of instruments. It seemed to be the quietest part of the island, and she was ready, finally, to get some rest for the night.

"Tomorrow," she said to Mabel and Mimi as she rubbed her eyes. "We will get this all figured out tomorrow."

CHAPTER THREE

UTOPIAN FALLS

That night, as Annalise slept, she dreamt that she, Mabel, and Mimi lived at the base of a huge pair of waterfalls. How they lived there, and why they did not get wet, she didn't know. She only knew that her life at the falls was the most pleasant existence she could have ever imagined because the constant sound of rushing water filled her head, cleaning away all the noise and worry that she hadn't even realized had lodged itself in there.

The falls were beautiful, too, both in themselves and because they were graced by a generous variety of mistbows. These were not rainbows, Annalise learned, because mist caused them, not rain, and, unlike rainbows, the mistbows were always there, or *perpetual*, as she heard other people at the falls say. The amazing thing was that all different sorts of these mistbows danced along the falls. Some of them were long while others were short, and some were wide while others were thin. There were twin and single bows, arched and straight bows, bows that looked like circles, and bows shaped with jagged edges, like flames. Yet as different as many of these bows were from each other, they all reflected one another in a merry wonderment of color, just as if a kaleidoscope had burst into the air.

The water itself fell over a horseshoe shaped ridge and plunged a very steep and long drop into the streambed. In this curved ridge, the waterfalls surged side-by-side, but not touching, leaving a thin strip of bare cliff in the middle that reminded Annalise of the part her mother used to comb into her hair before braiding it. And though the falls rushed with the force of millennia over the cliff, once they reached the bottom, they were a mere sheen, like glass, along the floor, and people walked directly on it as surely as if it had been solid ground. Now Annalise stood on this sheen, looking up at the falls in awe.

Mabel and Mimi stood beside her, smacking their lips.

"The air tastes so good here," Mabel said.

"I want to eat it," Mimi concurred.

"Oh, me, too, me, too," Annalise sang, twirling around in the streambed with her arms outstretched. "I love this dream!"

Lemon colored butterflies landed along her arms and on her nose as she twirled. Their wings made tinkling sounds with each flutter, and when they all fluttered together, they sounded like wind chimes.

Then, as suddenly as they had landed, they flew away all at once, creating a wavering, tinkling, yellow flag in the wind.

Annalise clapped her hands and exclaimed with joy, "I love butterflies. I just love them! Especially the kind that sound like wind chimes."

Mabel and Mimi gave her that look that her mother often gave her right before she said, "Why Annalise Alexia Humphrey, sometimes I think you are just full of it!"

It was what you would call a "pointed look."

Annalise self-consciously cleared her throat and said, "Well, at least now that I know about them, they're my favorites."

Soon a man ran by, trailing after the butterflies, and then came back and introduced himself as P.T. Marigold, Chaser of Butterflies.

"I take it you're newcomers," he said, stopping to talk.

"Yes. I'm Annalise of the Verdant Hills, and these are my friends, Mabel and Mimi."

"Nice to meet you all," P.T. said. And before Annalise knew what had happened, he'd begun a ramble. He said that the community at the falls lived a life of joy and serenity and that each person wanted the best for everyone, so they all agreed on everything. No one believed their own needs were more important than anyone else's, and no one thought other people's needs were more important than their own. Jealousy did not exist, and shame was so infrequent they barely remembered the word. He said if someone made a mistake, they didn't even try to hide it, because everyone else understood and forgave them instantly. He said his peoples' lack of negative emotions and attitudes freed up lots of time for butterfly chasing and other such important activities.

"How long will you stay?" he asked.

"We live here now," Annalise responded, surprising herself.

"Thought so," he said, straightening his marigold colored bowtie.

"Why?" Annalise asked.

"Why, indeed," P.T. Marigold, Chaser of Butterflies responded.

"No, I'm asking a question," Annalise said.

"Oh, I love questions," P.T Marigold responded. "I love asking them, I love answering them, I love posing them, and I love writing them down." He winked at Mabel and made a writing gesture with his hand.

Then, "Do you like questions?" he asked, turning to Annalise.

"I do," she said. "I do indeed. And, in fact, I have one."

"Well, why didn't you say so! What a delight. A true pleasure. Ask away."

"How can you tell we're newcomers?"

"Because you're just on the verge," he said.

"What do you mean 'on the verge'?" Annalise asked.

"At the brink," P.T. said "Like when the water is at the edge of the cliff, just about to fall over."

"I know what 'verge' means," Annalise said, with a slight giggle. "I meant, what am I on the verge of?"

"Reading my mind. Mental telepathy. Knowing my thoughts and feelings without having to use words. We can all do it here. You're just on the verge."

"Then what am I thinking?" Annalise challenged.

"You're wondering if we have cookies here, and fudge. You're hungry. You miss your mother, and you think I'm a funny man with a funny tie. Also, your sheep have a question. They think in unison, like twins. They want to know what I do with the butterflies when I catch them. But I don't catch them. I only chase them, and sometimes they chase me. Chasing is the fun part. There is no need for catching."

"But nothing makes sense here. How can you know about jealousy, for instance, if it doesn't exist?"

"Just because it doesn't exist here doesn't mean we don't know about it. We know about lots of things from other worlds."

Soon a friend of P.T.'s walked up. He wore a plaid green suit and a cap with a feather in it. He was only about three feet tall, but he was also three feet wide, so there was actually a substantial amount of him, lacking in height as he was.

"Good day, P.T. Marigold, Chaser of Butterflies," he said.

"Good day, Cosmo Skyler, Observer of Clouds." P.T. responded. "What's in the sky today?"

"Many shapes today, my friend, many glorious shapes. I've seen puckered lips, tangled hearts, frogs leaping, an entire family of cats, and a cow jumping over a moon. Beautiful weather we're having. And, oh, you've made new friends. Will you introduce me?"

"Sure, sure, Cosmo, old pal. This is Annalise of the Verdant Hills, and these are her sidekicks, Mabel and Mimi, the upright, talking wondersheep."

Mimi and Mabel crowded around Cosmo in excitement.

"Do you really always just look for shapes in the clouds?" Mimi asked.

"Do you sing to the clouds?" Mabel asked.

"And tell them stories?" Mimi said.

"Of course," Cosmo replied. "Doesn't everyone?"

A woman came along who said she didn't want to get pinned down to an activity such as cloud watching or butterfly chasing, so she made up a new one each month. She had drawn shapes in the water, been a professional petter of dogs and cats, paid visits to neighbors, walked to and fro, sat cross-legged in the grass, and taste-tested honeysuckle stems.

"Wow!" Annalise said. "What on earth do the kids study in school if the occupations are so widely varied? And how do you study cat petting, anyway?"

"Funny you should ask," the woman replied with a huge grin. "I myself have been a teacher in schools."

The woman began to spin around.

"Well, let's see … we teach twirling in circles."

She hopped over Annalise's feet.

"And hopping over feet."

She pulled a bottle from her purse and a wand from the bottle.

"We teach blowing bubbles."

The woman then began to prance around like royalty, after which she crouched down like a tiger.

"And we teach make-believe."

"But what about the basics?" Annalise asked.

"What are 'basics'?" the woman asked back.

"You know, math, science, language."

"Oh, yes, math!" the woman exclaimed. "It is ever so important to know how many petals are on a daisy or how many feathers on a bird. Do you ever wonder how many syllables are sung in the song you are singing, or how many sheep are in the herd?"

"Why, no," Mabel responded. "I never did wonder how many sheep there were, not until now, that is."

"Well, what do they use math for where you come from?" the woman asked.

"My mother uses it to balance her checkbook and pay her taxes," Annalise responded.

"Oh, no wonder you don't like it," the woman said. "You see, that's the good thing about not having money or taxes. Then you can use all of your counting energy to tally important things like how many friends you can fit into your house for a sleepover or how many puppies there are in a litter."

Just as Annalise was about to say that she quite agreed, she realized that she was no longer standing before the woman, but that she was instead suddenly walking along the streambed with a different woman, one who reminded her of her mother. She had sea-green eyes and light brown hair, the color of an autumn leaf.

"What happened?" Annalise asked her. "I was just talking to another woman and two funny little men. Now they're gone, and I'm walking with you."

"It's *your* dream, Annalise. You tell me what happened."

Annalise thought for a minute.

"Well, I was thinking about my mother," she said. "Then you appeared."

"Oh! Well, that explains it," the woman responded. "I'm a mother archetype."

"What's that?"

"It means I am a model of how people think of motherly qualities. I show up in lots of dreams, of course in different forms. "Ima Angel, at your service."

She made an elegant curtsey, and when she did, she looked down and caught her reflection in the sheen of water beneath her feet.

"Oh, Annalise, you imagined me so beautifully," she said.

They continued to walk along, and Ima said "hello" to the many people they passed. "Hello, Ima," they sometimes called back; other times they said things like, "What a pleasure to see you, sweet Ima."

Annalise noticed that when Ima looked at someone, she honored them with her eyes. It wasn't that she looked for a long time; her eyes just held a person closely, as if that person were receiving the attention of her entire being for the duration of the look. Ima didn't need to use her mouth to smile, either, because something inside her was always smiling. To Annalise, being looked at by Ima felt like being hugged without actually getting a hug, or like being told that you are wonderful without anyone using words.

"I know you miss her," Ima said. "She misses you, too."

"I want to see her," Annalise said.

Ima just nodded and smiled in a way that said everything would be all right.

She led Annalise to an exotic house made of bamboo stalks and roofed with flower petals. It was on a crag that jutted out just a short distance from the falls, and in the part of the house facing the falls, an enormous window protruded from the kitchen. Annalise could see people near the window, sitting on floor cushions around a table made out of a huge tree trunk. They were talking and drinking tea.

As Ima and Annalise approached the house, the people around the table got up and came to the door to greet them.

"Annalise," Ima said, "I would like you to meet my family. These are my twin sons, Dragos and Paxton, my daughter, Freddi, and this is my husband, Axil."

Annalise was surprised by how handsome Ima's teenaged sons were. They had sandy blond hair, and Dragos' hung just a bit over his left eye while Paxton's hung over his right, like a mirror image. They had strong jaws, and clefts in their chins, and when they smiled, it was like someone had turned on all the lights at a stadium.

Axil said, "Welcome," and Freddi, who was about Annalise's age, jumped forward and hugged her. Dragos and Paxton shook her hand, and then Paxton thanked her.

"Thank me? Why?" asked Annalise.

"You think we look like movie stars," Dragos said. "What are movie stars, by the way?"

"Something from her waking world," their father said. "We can talk about all that later. Let's just get Annalise fed for now."

They led her back to the kitchen, and when they sat down, Annalise noticed that the table was not *made from* a tree trunk but that it was an *actual* tree trunk with its roots still in the earth.

Dragos went over to the counter and headed back toward Annalise with a mug.

Annalise began, "Oh, I don't—"

"Drink tea," Dragos said. "I know. Steamed milk with a teaspoon of honey and three drops of vanilla extract."

"How did you know?"

"We just do," Dragos said. "You know that. Anyway, the sandwich will be ready in a minute."

"We're melting the cheese for you," Freddi said. "I like my cheese melted, too."

Soon Dragos brought Annalise's sandwich, and they sat at the table, talking and laughing. The twins horsed around a bit and tried to outdo each other telling jokes. They told Annalise they knew she was an excellent storyteller and that when she felt settled in they wanted her to tell them a story.

Annalise started to agree, but before she could say anything, something strange occurred. Right in the midst of the bustle, everything went stone silent. She could still see Paxton talking, but no sound came out, just like when you're watching a movie and you press "mute." Bob had appeared from nowhere and sat cross-legged in the center of the table with his eyes closed and his hands pressed together. Judging by the way everyone acted, Annalise quickly figured out that she was the only one who could see Bob and hear nothing. She decided to try some telepathy herself.

"Are you really there, Bob?" she thought.

"You tell me. It's your dream," Bob thought back.

"Where are my sheep?" Annalise thought. "I haven't seen them since I talked to P.T. and Cosmo."

"You don't need them right now. They'll come back when you need them," Bob replied. He was glowing more than ever.

"Why has everything gone mute?"

"It hasn't. You are just finally hearing the silence. The silence is always there, even around the sound. Listen to Paxton."

Suddenly the volume was back on, and Annalise listened to Paxton and noticed, for the first time, the silence surrounding every word he said, how it was there before the sounds, between the sounds and after the sounds. It was always there. It was just that sometimes sound was there, too.

Freddi laughed, and Annalise noticed that silence surrounded her laughter as well.

"Close your eyes," Bob instructed Annalise.

Annalise closed her eyes, and she saw an image of outer space—a huge blue-black expanse with twinkling stars.

"Do you see it?"

"Yes," Annalise thought back.

"Sounds are like stars twinkling in the vast silence from which they are born. They live and die, but silence is eternal and ever-present, just like space."

"I get it," Annalise thought. "I get it."

She opened her eyes, and Bob and the others were gone. The night sky had given way to a rising sun, and the field of instruments glistened with dewdrops and morning light. Annalise rose and stood to greet the day. She breathed deeply and stretched her arms high over her head. Around her lay instrument after instrument, as far as the eye could see, and right next to her, in a small, soft clearing, lay her two adorable, snoring sheep.

"Mabel, Mimi," she said, crouching between them and nudging them gently. "Wake up. I think I have an idea."

CHAPTER FOUR

SWAN SONG

Mabel and Mimi reluctantly trailed behind Annalise, who led them back to the beach. They dragged their feet and stopped frequently to catch their breath. As they got closer to the noise, they bent down and picked flowers and stuffed them in their ears to try to muffle the sound. What a sight they were: Two sheep walking upright, with bright orange flowers sticking out of their ears!

But, like everything else that grew on the island, these flowers turned out to be instruments—bells, to be precise. And with every step Mabel and Mimi took, the flowerbells chimed.

"I should have known," Mabel said, pulling the flowers from her ears and tossing them to the ground.

"Me, too!" Mimi said, throwing hers down, as well.

They continued on their mission, ears unprotected, and as they got closer to the beach, the musicians came into focus. Apparently, they had no more need of sleep than they did of sustenance. They were in the exact same spots they had been in the day before, and they sounded the same, too, only louder, if that were possible.

Without hesitation, Annalise marched headlong into the noise like a fearless soldier. Her jaw was set, her shoulders squared, and her eyes intense. Determination surged through her little body like electricity through a wire.

"Come on, sheep, keep it moving," she called over her shoulder as she climbed atop a big black piano. She turned her back to the wide, blue ocean, and, just as she'd hoped, she saw a panoramic view of all the musicians on the beach playing in their various groups.

Mabel and Mimi caught up and stood in front of the piano.

"What now?" Mabel asked.

"Just relax," Annalise replied.

"Relax?" Mimi asked, dumbfounded.

"And be as quiet as possible," Annalise added with an air of self-importance.

"We practically ran all this way to just wait and be quiet?" Mabel asked.

"Yes," Annalise said. "Just until something changes. Please trust me. I'm not sure exactly how all this will work. I just know that it will."

Mabel and Mimi nodded their heads and curled up beside the piano legs with their eyes closed. Even though they had just woken up, a morning nap seemed like a good idea after their hike across the island.

Annalise was no longer looking at the sheep, and while they settled in to sleep, she stood on top of the piano and listened. She needed time to explore, to figure things out. She closed her eyes and opened her ears and concentrated with deep intensity. What she heard was noise that overlapped and tangled in on itself like a sticky sonic web from which there seemed no escape. She imagined the musicians with spider bodies and human heads, spinning this noise from their abdomens and chasing after her with instruments that were also weapons. Then she got scared and quickly opened her eyes to make sure the musicians were not actually spiders. She looked down at Mabel and Mimi. They were asleep and snoring.

"Oh, for goodness sake! Those sheep can sleep anywhere," she said. "If they can find peace in all this noise, so can I."

Still standing on top of the big black piano, she closed her eyes again, and this time she just plain listened. Every other time she had heard the musicians, she realized, all she had done was try to figure out how to get them to quit playing. Now she listened with no other thought in mind but to hear their music the best she could, despite its chaos.

She dropped her hands down by her sides and let her jaw muscles relax. She wasn't concentrating anymore. She was just letting everything happen naturally. The sounds began to separate out, and even though all the musicians played at the same time, she heard each group's song distinct from the noise, as if there were space between the songs that hadn't been there before. She began to actually enjoy the music. It was kind of like a word find puzzle. The overall impression was of chaos, but within that disorder were clusters of meaning.

Annalise then noticed something even more extraordinary: that she could hear each instrument individually, and then, finally, each *note* individually. Around and between each of the notes, there was silence, glorious, beautiful silence. And in this silence Annalise took shelter. It was like she was floating on her back in the ocean, gently rocked to and fro by waves of quiet. And as she listened to the space between the notes, she gradually came to realize that the sound had stopped altogether. The musicians were no longer playing.

She opened her eyes and saw them walking forward and gathering around the piano. They were not even speaking to each other, much less playing their instruments. They were standing together in silence. Real and true silence! Annalise had done it. Her own calmness had quieted the musicians and drawn them toward her.

She held her baton poised in the air, perfectly still. Then she heard an echo in her head. It said, "You'll know what to do when the time comes. Oh, and by the way, the time has come."

It was Bob.

Annalise lowered her baton ever so slightly, and the musicians played a perfectly synchronized note. She held her baton still again, and the musicians held the note. She had found the silence. Now she just needed to find the song.

Annalise thought of her mother singing to her before bedtime. She let her baton glide through the air like the wing of a swan in flight, realizing that her mother's bedtime songs had always been the music of swans rising from silence to quiet her mind and lull her to sleep. She knew, also, that these musicians, once such ugly ducklings of sound, were now the swans, and it was up to her baton to lift them into the air. She was the only wing they had.

Her body moved without thought. The wisdom was stored there, in her bones. It was the music of her mother, and Annalise just let it pass into her baton on its own. She felt a warm electricity surge through her body, and then, like the wild swans of destiny, the music lifted into the sky and soared above the ocean.

The web that she had imagined earlier, the one that had frightened her, reappeared in her mind's eye. Only this time the web wasn't scary. Now the web connected everything powerful and beautiful in the universe to every other powerful and beautiful thing. It didn't tangle in upon itself as it had before, but, instead, regained the breezy spaces between strands. Annalise imagined that by hopping on one of those strands she could slide to anywhere she wanted to be. The music would take her there.

Mimi woke up and nudged Mabel.

"Mabel, Mabel dear. Look at Annalise. She's conducting the musicians. She did it, and we slept through the whole thing just like a couple of silly sheep."

"Oh, yes, Mimi. It's glorious. Oh, and we missed all the excitement. I bet she really told them off."

"Yeah," said Mimi. "I bet she really let them have it!"

The sheep gave each other a high five, or one, or whatever it is when you have hooves instead of fingers, and they danced joyously along the shoreline, where they kicked the water and cleared their throats of the raspy remnants of sleep.

After all, they wanted to be prepared for backup singing, should the need arise.

CHAPTER FIVE

THE AWARD CEREMONY

Annalise felt caught on a wind, as though she were riding the musical notes up into the heavens. She felt lighter, weightless even, and, in very little time at all, she discovered that she'd begun to float upwards, back to the land of clouds, her two sheep floating alongside her.

"Well, well, Calypso finally released you, I see," came the familiar, screeching voice. "You must have passed a test or something. Oh, don't tell me. Don't say anything. Let me guess. Did you pull a sword from a stone or answer an ancient riddle? Win an archery contest? Or maybe you wrestled a wild boar to the ground? Oh dang it, no, there are no boars around here. Think Hagski, think. Oh, I've got it. I've got it!"

Annalise heard Hagski rustle through some papers before continuing her barrage of questions.

"Did you agree to a Mount Moriah sacrifice? Oh, yeah, right, like you're old enough to have children to sacrifice. What are you doing, trying to throw me off track? I bet you killed and skinned the Nemean lion? Well, if that's what you're trying to imply, I know you're full of it because you're too skinny for such a task. Something less physical, then. Did you find the golden apples or the Golden Fleece? Don't say. Let me guess. Which was it? How many tasks did you complete? How many tests did you pass? Tell me. Come on. Out with it, girl. What? Has the cat got your tongue? Did someone staple your lips together while you were asleep? Have you suddenly gone mute? *Can you hear me?"*

"You haven't paused for her to answer," Mabel said, curling her lips into a scowl.

"Yeah, and you told her not to answer anyway," said Mimi.

"That was before. I'm ready now. Spit it out. The suspense is killing me."

Hagski appeared before them, looking as disheveled as ever. This time she had on professional attire: a tan skirt and jacket with a button down white and tan striped shirt. The shirt was untucked and missing buttons, and both the jacket and skirt had stains in a variety of shades. Her pantyhose were torn, and she seemed to be missing a heel from one of her shoes. She pressed her face right up to Annalise's, nose to nose.

"Well, then, come on child. Out with it!"

"I did pass a test, I guess," said Annalise. "I got all the musicians on Acoustic Island to play together."

"That's it?" screeched Hagski. "Well, I suppose you're proud of yourself now. I bet you'll be congratulating yourself for days, strutting around like some kind of deranged peacock. I bet you've already told everyone you know. Maybe you're even expecting a trophy or some kind of award. Is that all it's about for you, getting the award? Fine. Well, what do you want then? Let's see."

Hagski flipped open the flap of a tattered, tan briefcase and began to rummage through it. The image was similar to that of a magician pulling a rabbit, a table, and a vase of flowers out of a hat. Various items poked over the top of the soft leather opening, and there was no way those items could have fit into the briefcase. Annalise saw a kangaroo, a piano, a dining room table, a toilet, and a police officer with a whistle to his lips. There was also a hockey team and a herd of antelope.

"I have a Caldecott, a Nobel, a Leonardo da Vinci Award, a

Newberry, a medallion from a spelling bee, an Academy Award, a Bharat Ratna, an Olympic Medal for synchronized swimming, an NEA Grant, a Heisman, an American Music Award, an Italian Music Award, a Japanese Music Award for Best Singer, an Emmy, an FIFA World Cup Trophy, an Adriano González León Biennial Novel Prize, a PADI Diving Award, and a Pulitzer Prize."

Annalise began to say that she didn't need an award, but Hagski interrupted her with a dramatic throat clearing. She then gave Annalise a pointed look and began digging through her bag again.

"I have a Lombardi, a prix Interallié, a MacArthur, a Hong Kong Film Award for Best Director, an MVP, a Prince of Wales Trophy, a Golden Shoe, an Aviva Art Award, a Sidney Myer Fund Australian Ceramic Art Award, a Stanley Cup, a Chess Oscar, an Edith Cummings Munson Golf Award, a Church of Iceland Award, a Grand Prix, and a blue ribbon from a state fair."

Hagski looked up from her bag at Annalise, and Annalise smiled dumbly. She didn't know what Hagski would do next, whether or not she was done digging through her bag, or if she was about to launch into another monologue.

There was a moment of awkward silence, not the grand and glorious silence Annalise had enjoyed in her dream at the waterfalls and on Acoustic Island, but the kind of silence when something is supposed to be said but no one is saying it.

"What? Cat got your tongue again, girl? You are the strangest creature, speaking when you're not supposed to, silent when you should speak. Didn't you get any home training?"

"Pardon me," Annalise said. "I was just trying to say that I don't need an award. The satisfaction of a job well done is good enough for me."

"Oh, I see how it is. Smug little thing, ain't ya? Well, you'd better snap out of it. The tests are only going to get harder and harder, little Miss Smarty-pants. Eventually you won't be able to pass them, and you'll wish you had something to hang onto, some proof of your former victories."

"Really, it's okay," Annalise said.

Mabel and Mimi exchanged glances.

"You *must* choose," Hagski screeched. "I cannot choose for you. Come on, girl. Step up to the plate. Do what you know is right. Take a chance for once."

"Well, um, I guess I'll take a Grammy Award then."

The look on Hagski's face said that she would probably like to hit Annalise over the head with her briefcase.

Annalise flinched a bit in anticipation.

"*Excuse* me. Did I say I have a Grammy Award? Does it look like I have a Grammy? Does it even look like my bag is big enough to have a Gramophone in it?"

"Oh, well, I guess not. No problem. I'll take the American Music Award then."

"Well, have you ever heard of the likes of that?" Hagski asked, turning slightly to her left to face an equally disheveled companion who had appeared suddenly from nowhere.

"*Settling* for an American Music Award?" Hagski said, turning toward the new person. "Just a *mere* American Music Award for Miss Fancypants. How will she ever survive?"

Hagski flipped her multi-colored hair over her shoulder and made an indignant "hmmmmph" sound.

"Guess she'll just have to make do, Hagski-poo. Maybe she'll just put it on a high shelf. Maybe she'll hide it behind a more prestigious award, like the participation trophy from her second grade dance recital. Maybe, over time, she will realize that the AMA is at least better than no award at all."

"Ladies," came the voice of Me Anyou from behind a cloud, "you sound like a couple of monkeys rattling around inside a skull. Leave this poor girl alone, and let her claim her rightful award."

"Which is?" Hagski asked.

"The next step of her journey," Bob said, appearing before them.

CHAPTER SIX

HULAN HOUSE

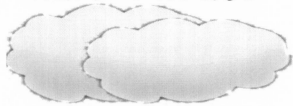

Annalise squealed with delight when she saw that Bob had arrived to lead her to her next destination. Although he was only a Light man and had no real physical substance, he wore moccasins, a loincloth, and a Native American headdress with tall feathers and dangling beads. From his mouth protruded a small pipe with an unusual, dry smelling tobacco.

"Follow me," Bob said, forming the words around the pipe.

Annalise did not ask where. She followed Bob as he hopped lightly from cloud to cloud, barely landing on one before he sprung to the next.

"It seems like we're going faster this time," Annalise said.

"Faster indeed," said Mimi, panting behind her.

"Like streaks of light," said Mabel.

"Move your feet, not your mouths, kiddos," said Bob, "and you will go faster, like me."

As he leapt, smoke trailed behind him, twisting into a curly corkscrew, and then straightening out and twisting around again. Cloud after cloud, Annalise felt herself moving more quickly toward some unknown destination that wavered in the distance through a haze of dust, smoke, and mirage. Annalise could see people dancing, the dust swirling around their heels as they stomped the ground. Beside the dancers was a large building, much bigger than a house. It was the same color as the ground, a sun burnt beige.

The dancers had long black hair, which hung braided down their backs, and they wore black ponchos with blocky, brightly colored designs. It was hard for Annalise to make much else out, but as she got closer to the moving figures, the clouds began to disappear, and soon there was nothing but sun and open sky and the tops of dry, dusty mountains on which to leap, one after another.

"It's called adobe," Bob said.

Annalise noticed that Bob's earlier statement about talking and leaping was correct. When he spoke, it did slow him down considerably.

"What?"

"You're wondering why their pueblo is the same color as the ground. It's called adobe. They make it by mixing straw, clay and water. Very durable. Very cheap. Ecologically sound."

"Great. That's really neat," Annalise said, trying not to wonder about anything else since she wanted Bob to keep hopping as fast as he had been before.

"Wondering is worth the slowing down it takes," Bob said. "Promise you'll keep wondering."

"Yes. You're right. I promise," Annalise said, hopping to the next mountaintop. She could see a man in the distance. The scene still wavered, but it was much clearer than it had been before. The man had separated himself from the dancers, and he waved to Bob, both hands spread around his head the way someone might show an airplane where to land.

Bob responded with a huge "hello," and soon the foursome was standing directly in front of the man, beside the pueblo, surrounded by dancers. The man and Bob pressed the palms of their hands together, and Annalise guessed that they had greeted each other this way many times.

Bob then turned to the dancers and thanked them. He told Annalise that they had been dancing to create a vibration, one that would lead Bob to them. He said they could also use drums or other methods, too, and that as long as they got the frequency right, he could find them.

"We've been waiting," the man said. "We knew you were coming, but we didn't know exactly when, and we weren't sure just who you would have with you. Two sleeps ago, Kána dreamt of your coming, and woke everyone up. We've been dancing for twenty hours now. What an unexpected delight to find that you've brought a child and some sheep. Is this little girl who I think she is?"

"Yes, my wunderkind. She travels with her own totems," Bob said.

"Two of the same," the man replied. "It's a strong connection. They will stay a while?"

"Yes, and I'll be around," Bob said. "If you need me, just send the vibration."

They touched palms again, and Bob turned to Annalise.

"Annalise," he said, "I'm going now, but I want you to understand that this man is a shaman, a medicine man priest gifted with the power to help others heal their bodies, spirits and minds. His mother, Kána, is also the tribal mother, and, some say, the greatest healer who has ever lived. You can trust them like family."

Annalise looked at the man, who was dressed in garb similar to Bob's. He looked like the Native Americans she had seen in her textbooks at school. He was an exceptionally large man. His cheekbones were high, his nose prominent, and, like the rivers and streets of a map, his wrinkles wended their way over the hills and valleys of his face.

Annalise asked where Kána was.

"She's resting," the man said. "She danced for many hours this morning."

"I'd like to meet her before you go," Annalise said, turning back to Bob.

"Of course, my dear," Bob replied. "I didn't even think of it. You certainly must feel comfortable, or I will not consider leaving. I'll fetch her from the pueblo at once."

He turned and dashed off.

As they waited, the shaman studied Annalise as intensely as she had been studying him. The dancers began to move closer as well, also inspecting Annalise, Mabel, and Mimi.

"You are not at the beginning of your journey," the shaman said to Annalise. As he spoke, he looked into her eyes in a way that reminded her of a doctor examining her pupils.

"You've been to the land of the falls," he said.

"But how did you—"

"And you two are continuing beyond her," he said, looking at Mabel and Mimi in the same way.

"What? Continuing beyond me? Where?"

"Not now. Much, much later," Mimi responded. "Don't worry about it right now, Annalise. It's okay."

The shaman seemed to feel that he had sufficiently assessed the situation, and, making a slight bow to Annalise and the sheep, he said, "Welcome to the Hulan House. You may call me Tony."

Mabel balked.

"May *call you* Tony?" Mimi had dealt with Hagski so often since acquiring language that she knew to not leave any room for doubt, misinterpretation or indecision. "Is it your name or not? After all, we could *call you* anything, whether it was your name or just some random word."

"Such a passion for clarity. Brilliant!" Tony said.

His eyes sparkled a deep appreciation for Mimi and her very specific question. "Tony is a nickname I offer because you most likely cannot pronounce my real name."

The look on Mimi's face made it clear she thought Tony had

accused her of being something akin to a single celled amoeba or a fossilized, prehistoric turd.

She sat back on her haunches and crossed her front hooves over her chest with an air of indignation.

Tony, who was quite perceptive, understood immediately that he'd hurt Mimi's pride about her language skills.

"What I mean is not that you would have a hard time due to your recent acquisition of language, but that *anyone* outside of the tribe might have difficulty with the pronunciation. Our language is very different from the one you and Annalise and Mabel speak."

But Tony's attempt to make amends did not work. Not only did Mimi continue to glare at him, but now Mabel was glaring at him, too.

"You might just tell them your name," Annalise said, with a slight chuckle in her voice. She remembered from her lessons at school that Native American names could be quite difficult to pronounce, and she knew Mabel and Mimi were in for a shock. But she also knew how stubborn they were.

"Okay, let's give it a try," Tony said. "It's Ixtxypzxxzxztw muazn qxytyqpz."

Mabel and Mimi's eyes widened.

"Well, in that case, it's nice to meet you, Tony," Mimi replied, extending her hoof to shake a greeting.

"Nice to meet you, too," Tony said, laughing.

Just then Bob returned with an older, smaller, female version of Tony. Annalise's worries that the woman would be annoyed at being awoken from her nap were completely unfounded. The woman grinned ear to ear, and, despite her age, practically sprinted toward Annalise.

"Welcome, dears, welcome!" she hollered, as loudly as you would to someone you thought was half-deaf. "I'm so glad you're here."

When she got close enough, she held both her hands out to

Annalise and said, "Dear child, I am Kána. I'm delighted to meet you."

As she waited for Annalise to introduce herself and her sheep, she continued to hold Annalise's hands in her own. It reminded Annalise of when she used to visit her grandmother's house and her grandmother would hold her hand and ask questions about her life: how school was going, what her favorite books and songs were, if she liked her teachers, what kinds of games she liked to play at recess. She would even ask about things she already knew, like Annalise's favorite color. She said people's tastes change with time, and she wanted to make sure she had the most recent updates. She was always interested in everything about Annalise, and Annalise could tell Kána was interested in her like that, too.

"I'm Annalise, and these are my friends Mabel and Mimi," Annalise said. "We're very pleased to meet you, as well."

"Indeed," said Mabel.

"Undoubtedly," said Mimi.

Kána released Annalise's hand and held Mabel's hoof and then Mimi's. "Very pleased to meet you, dears," she said. "How about a meal? You gals must be hungry after all that mountain hopping."

"That would be wonderful," the sheep chimed in unison.

Annalise gave Bob a thumbs up to let him know everything was okay, and Bob said a general goodbye to the group, turned on his heel, and was soon no more than a streak of light on a distant mountaintop.

Tony led Annalise, Mabel, and Mimi inside the adobe building to a room with long, wooden, picnic-style tables that had alternating bright red and yellow placemats. In the center of each table sat a huge, royal blue vase full of sunflowers, alongside several bowls of blueberries sprinkled with sugar.

The smoky smell of pinto beans wafted through the room, and a server ladled a chunky stew into big blue bowls before topping off each steaming bowl with a hunk of buttery cornbread.

"Just salad for me," Mabel said when she got to the front of the line.

"Me, too," said Mimi. "We're vegan."

They ate picnic style, with lots of commotion, boisterous talk, and people bobbing up and down to get more food whenever they pleased.

After dinner, Kána and Tony took Mabel, Mimi, and Annalise to a sitting room with a fireplace, beautiful red rugs, and soft beige couches. Each couch had an abundance of fluffy pillows and several blankets in a variety of colors thrown over the backs and arms. The rich smell of cedar incense drifted down from the mantle, and on the walls hung generations of black and white photos in simple wooden frames. Annalise thought if the room could speak words, it would have said, "Settle in. Stay a while."

Tony walked over to the fireplace and pulled a tea kettle off a hook, and, as he did, Annalise noticed a large gray rock in the corner of the room, next to the fireplace. It was big enough that three or four people could sit on it at a time.

"Milk, with herbs, sugar, and spices," Tony said, nodding toward the teacups that sat on the coffee table. Annalise held hers up so he could pour some milk for her, and Mabel and Mimi did the same.

"How do you like our petroglyph?" Kána asked as Tony filled Annalise's teacup.

"Petro-what?" Annalise asked.

"I saw you noticing the petro*glyph*," Kána said. "The rock with the carvings. Our people found it hundreds of years ago when they settled here. We built the pueblo around it to signify its importance to our community. It acts as a portal to other worlds."

"Well, it's an awfully nice rock," Annalise said. "Very large and distinguished looking. Really the best I've ever seen." She squinted her eyes at Kána, deciding whether or not to say what she wanted to say next. Then, concluding that it was okay, she said, "This milk is really weird, though. It doesn't taste like normal milk."

"Do you like it?" Tony wanted to know.

"Yes, very much."

"It's not the kind of milk you usually drink. It comes from a plant instead of a cow," Kána said.

"Did you mix in cinnamon?"

"Yes. Among other things," Kána replied.

"Tasty," Annalise said, leaning her head back into one of the big, fluffy pillows. She felt drowsy, so she decided to just listen for a bit while Mabel and Mimi told Kána and Tony about their adventures in the sky and on Acoustic Island. They started from the beginning, in the Verdant Hills, explaining how it rained and rained until they thought it would never stop.

Their voices took on a hushed, murmuring quality in the warmth of the firelit room, and Annalise began to feel entranced by the dancing shadows cast on the walls by the flickering flames. She stared at one of the walls and thought about a word Kána had used when telling her about the petroglyph, the word "portal." She remembered it from the fairy tales her mother had read her about kingdoms and palaces in faraway lands. She remembered that a "portal" was a door or entrance. But what had Kána said? To other worlds? Annalise's mind could barely grasp it. All the portals she and her mother had read about were entrances to fairy castles, or gates between kingdoms. That had seemed fantastical enough. But to other *worlds*?

It seemed too amazing to be true.

It was funny how the locations in the stories still seemed so exotic even after she had visited so many unusual places with Mabel and Mimi. The hold of imagination, Annalise realized, was as persistent as reality; once Annalise had pictured the settings and characters in the stories her mother read, they were in her mind forever. And the stories themselves, she mused, were portals to other worlds. So why not a rock, a petroglyph, with ancient stories carved upon it?

Yes, a rock could be a portal, too.

Annalise wasn't entirely sure whether she was asleep or awake. She felt her eyelids flutter, and she started to tell the sheep she was ready for bed, but before she could get the words out, she began to feel the most curious sensation: a low vibration, or hum, coming from the direction of the petroglyph.

CHAPTER SEVEN
THE PORTAL

"Don't be afraid," Kána said, leaning over Annalise's face and wiping her forehead with a cool, damp cloth. "The images you see may seem frightening, but you're safe, and they'll help you understand your journey. That's why Bob brought you here."

Annalise nodded and smiled.

"I understand," she said.

The room began to fade, and Annalise could faintly see that the dancers from outside the pueblo had come in and were dancing and singing with Mabel and Mimi.

"It's a prayer," Tony said. "They sing for your safe return. They dance the vibration that calls to you alone. When you're ready, close your eyes and breathe deeply from your belly. You will feel the vibration there, in your core. Let it lead you back to us."

Annalise nodded again, but she was slipping away. The call of the petroglyph was strong, and she could feel it pulling her toward the nighttime world of dreams.

Soon the room fell dark, and Annalise wasn't sure if the room itself had gone dim or if her eyes were just closed. What she could discern were small, dancing rectangles of light. All around her they jumped and flashed, disappeared and reappeared, twirled and spun in a dizzying array. Among them, she knew, was the portal she must enter, but there were tricksters as well.

This was no easy doorway, arched and waiting, with a simple knob to turn. No, Annalise had to catch and enter the correct portal out of the hundreds that flashed before her eyes. It seemed a frustrating and even impossible task, and just as she was about to give up, she noticed something about one of the portals, a slightly different shape - yes, it was more like an eye than a rectangle. It winked at her, and then she heard a laugh and an echoing voice.

"The time has come," it said.

It sounded like Me Anyou.

Annalise stared the eye down the way you would in a staring contest, never letting it out of her sight, never blinking or looking away, noticing nothing else at all in her peripheral vision. She stared at the eye like it was the only thing in the whole world, and her only purpose in life was to view it. She thought of nothing else, felt nothing else, perceived nothing else. It was just Annalise and the eye, the eye and Annalise.

"I've got you," she said.

But just then, the eye transformed into a rectangle, indistinguishable from all the other rectangles, and began to dance and flit around.

Annalise was crestfallen. She'd lost it, the portal to her important, albeit unknown, destination. She started to hum and sing to herself, because it was what always made her feel better, even without the sheep.

> La la la la
> la la la le
> alone in a void
> a dark scary void
> la la la la
> la la la le
> just the darkness
> a big scary eye
> dancing rectangles and me

la la la la
la la la le
la la la la
la la la le

Soon she could think of nothing else to sing, because when you're in a void like that, sometimes your mind is a void too. But then, luckily, something happened before she had to try to think of more words to sing. The rectangle that had been an eye separated itself out from the mass again and turned into a majestic bird that flew gracefully among the many darting rectangles, stretching its wings and showing off its dives and loops. It cawed at her, and she cawed back, instinctively understanding what it was offering.

"Yes, I want a ride," she said. "I'm going somewhere very important, and I must make haste. Come down, and I will climb upon your back, pretty bird."

The bird flapped its long, wide wings at her, and a feather drifted down, slowly, slowly. Annalise reached her hand out and let it fall onto her palm.

"How beautiful," she said, examining the feather.

She looked back up, but the bird was gone, and nothing remained but rectangles, dancing and leaping about her whole field of vision.

"Next time, I'm not going to let it get away," Annalise said, looking upwards for the eye or the bird or whatever else might appear.

And because something new had happened, she was able to make up new words for the song she sang to herself:

A big black bird
la la la la
la la la le
I'm just here
wherever I am
la la la la

la la la le
I'm not afraid
la la la la

She continued to look around, and she noticed, once again, a rectangle separating itself out from the rest. It moved closer and closer until Annalise could see that it was not just a rectangle. It was a long corridor that seemed to have no end.

Suddenly, without thinking about it at all, she ran forward and leapt straight into the corridor before it could get away or turn back into a plain rectangle.

"I'm in," she screamed.

"I'm in. I'm in. I'm in."

She landed on her bottom but stood up and brushed off quickly, as her mother had taught her to do after a fall. She felt anxious to see what lay at the end of the hallway, so she put one foot in front of the other and began a fast-paced walk.

Look at all the gray speckles on this hard, white floor, she thought. And look at the white walls and the white ceilings, and, oh, there's an elevator. Should I take the elevator?

She was beginning to get the impression that she'd leapt into an overly sterile environment. Everything seemed scrubbed clean, even the floors. And the corridor actually smelled lemony, the way her school smelled when she first arrived in the mornings.

As she continued to walk, she noticed other hallways jutting off the main hallway, and as she wandered and weaved, she discovered that down those hallways were more hallways and more elevators, and down those hallways were even more hallways. It seemed, in fact, that the entire world Annalise had just entered was comprised of nothing more than hallways and elevators, one after the other for as far as the eye could see.

Well, I'm just in a big maze, she thought. I know Kána said everything would be okay, but I'm still a little nervous.

She decided that thinking too much was not a good idea right now and that it was better to instead use her instincts, so she just let her feet go where they wanted. It was like when her Mom hid a present from her, and she had to find it with nothing more than her mother's voice calling out "warmer" and "cooler." Only on this hunt there was no voice. Her feet just thought "warm" and "cool" on their own.

She turned left, then right, right again, then left, left, left, right. Trying not to think about how much everything looked the same, she went up two floors in an elevator until the lighted number told her she was at the tenth floor. When the elevator stopped, she got out and went left, left, right, and then past a little lobby with people sitting in chairs.

People sitting in chairs. Much warmer, she thought, surprised to realize she'd been thinking about searching for gifts the whole time her feet had been navigating the maze.

She continued walking, and then, just past a potted plant with furry purple and green leaves, she turned left again, then right, and headed down a hallway that seemed longer than the others, finally turning left again, and next making one last right.

Then, what do you know, *boom*. Just to her left, she saw an actual door, with an actual doorknob, and she laughed out loud. It couldn't have been plainer: simple, gray, with a round, silver knob. The portal itself, it turned out, would be easy after all. It was just the getting to it that was complicated.

Annalise put her hand on the knob, ready to turn, but it didn't move when she twisted her wrist. Instead, her hand passed clear through the door so that her forearm and hand were on the other side of it, while her elbow, upper arm, and shoulder were on the same side as her body.

How strange, Annalise thought. Part of me is in here, and part of me is in there. I must figure out how to get all of me in there.

She put her foot through the door also, just to see if it would go, and it did.

"I don't think I'm made of meat here," she said aloud, thinking of how Hagski had once asked whether she was made of meat or vegetable.

"I'm not made of vegetable, either," she added, just to be clear.

She wasn't sure who she was talking to. There was no one visible, but, as she had discovered already, not seeing someone certainly didn't mean someone wasn't listening.

She pushed her whole leg through the door.

"I think I might be made of air," she said. "Just plain air."

And with that, she slipped right through the door to the other side, without even having to open it.

Or perhaps the *door* is made of air, Annalise thought. It's hard to know just what things are made of when the laws of science have changed all up on you and people can walk through doors without opening them.

Annalise soon realized that she had entered into an actual room instead of another hallway or corridor.

"Oh, happy day," she said. "Maybe I'm somewhere where I can just sit down and think for a minute."

She walked over to a little round table that had two chairs pulled up to it, sat down in one of them and began to examine the items lying on top of the table.

"Hmmmmm," she mused. "A coffee cup, a packet that says 'Chamomile,' three one dollar bills, a quarter, two shiny pennies, a set of nesting dolls lined in a row, a vase of flowers, a small stuffed bear with button eyes, a hairbrush, and, finally, two books: *The Lost Princess of Oz* – a favorite – and *The Tibetan Book of Living and Dying* – whatever that is."

Annalise picked up the hairbrush, which reminded her of her mother's because it was silver with roses etched onto the back, and began to run strokes through her hair while she thought about what to do next. She wasn't used to exploring strange places without Mabel and Mimi, and she felt a little lonely and confused.

I'm so glad to be somewhere instead of just on the way to somewhere like I was before, she thought, and she continued to brush her hair while she looked around the room.

On a shelf behind her was another vase of flowers, and, beside that, some balloons with giraffes and clowns on them. One of the balloons said, "Get Well Soon," and another one said, "Godspeed Your Recovery." There were cards propped up all along the shelf, with pretty pictures of flowers and streams and rainbows on the covers of them, and above the shelf a painting hung on the wall. It was the same as the painting in Annalise's own bedroom at home: an outdoor flower market with basket after basket, table after table of brightly colored flowers. The painting had once hung in the family's dining room, but Annalise loved it so much that her mother had moved it to her bedroom, right across from her bed, so that she could see it first thing when she woke up each morning.

"What a funny coincidence," Annalise said as she continued to examine the room.

Then, high in the corner, above her head, she noticed a television set that was off. She reached up to turn it on, and when she did, she was startled to see in the reflection that there was a woman sitting in a chair just a few feet away from her.

How had Annalise not noticed the woman before? She sat there, plain as day, solid as the TV that reflected her image. Her feet were planted on the ground, her posture was firm, and her hands were on her knees. She looked straight ahead, as if in a trance, and she seemed to be mouthing words to herself, but she was not speaking aloud.

Annalise ran over and stood in front of her.

Why, this woman looks just like my mother, Annalise realized. But she's a little skinner, and she doesn't look as healthy, and her eyes are so red.

"Are you a mother archetype?" she asked the woman, but the woman didn't answer or even appear to see her.

Now that Annalise was closer, she could see that the woman had tears in her eyes and on her cheeks. She didn't sob, and was, in fact, so quiet that you'd need to be right up next to her to see that she was crying.

"Oh, please don't cry," Annalise said, moving closer so that she could wipe the woman's cheek. However, before she could get there, the woman startled her by speaking.

"Darling, if you can hear me, please give me a sign. There are so many things I want to say. Please don't be afraid. Even if you've lost your body. This isn't the end."

The woman got up and walked over to a bed with a child in it. There were bandages around the child's head and face, and the child's legs were elevated and in a cast. With all the bandaging, it was impossible to tell just who the child was, but Annalise had a pretty good idea.

"Mom, Mom. I'm here, behind you," she said.

She placed her hand on top of the woman's, which was on top of the child's, but her own hand had no substance and passed through the other two just as it had passed through the door knob before. The child's hand twitched.

"I knew you could hear me," the woman said, a fresh stream of tears running down her face.

"Listen, sweetheart. This is very important," she said. "You see, I'd be lying if I didn't admit that I want you to come back to me, but what is most important is that I want you to do what's right for you."

She paused for a minute, as if it took great effort to make this speech. Then she continued.

"Do you understand? I'm giving you permission, *my blessing* to do whatever you need to do, to make whatever choice you need to make." At this, the woman finally let out a full, heartfelt sob. "I didn't handle things properly with your father. I see that now, how difficult I must have made the transition. I want you to be at peace, to have no lingering doubts or fears. I love you so very much. I cherish you, and I **am** waiting, but you *do not* have to hang on for me."

The child's hand twitched again.

"Mom, I can hear you, and I love you, too," Annalise said. "I want to come back, but I don't know how yet. There's nothing to me. When I try to touch things, I don't stick."

Annalise heard her mom's voice again, but this time her mother didn't speak the words aloud. They were inside Annalise's head, as Bob's had been before.

"How can I help?" she asked.

Annalise surprised herself with an immediate rush of answers: "Music, mom. Play music in this room. Keep reading aloud. Pray. Meditate. Stay. Keep holding hands."

"Where are you?"

"I don't know. I might be here, but I might be at the Pueblo. Possibly both. Or neither."

"Pueblo?"

Annalise tried to find a way to explain, but suddenly she felt tired. She tried to lie down on the bed, to fill herself into the child, but, again, she didn't stick.

She felt herself being drawn, pulled back by the vibration at the pueblo.

"Bye, Mom. I'm so sorry. I tried to stay. I mean, I really, really wanted to stay. Really. Oh, no – I'm so, so sorry. I just can't … hang on."

She could feel her mother's concern.

"Don't worry. It's safe where I go. I'm sorry. I'll try to come back."

"No apologies," she heard. "No guilt. I'll be here."

And she drifted off and away, back to the sound of rustling clothes and moving feet, back to the strange, thick harmony of pueblo voices. They waited for her, welcomed her, like a beacon in a swirl of fog, like a light in the window on a cold day.

CHAPTER EIGHT

WEBMAP

When Annalise came to, she saw the fuzzy, wrinkled image of Kána's face hovering above her own. As it gradually came into focus, she felt the damp cloth still wiping her brow. Kána murmured in gentle, hushed tones not to be afraid, that everything would be all right, and Annalise had the impression of having been asleep for only a minute, even though her journey into the portal seemed to have lasted hours. She sat up and looked around the firelit room, taking in, once again, the flickering flames, the warm rugs, the throws over the couches, the petroglyph.

"I don't know if I'm asleep or awake," she said to Kána. "I've been through so many layers. Dreams inside dreams inside dreams. I'm like one of those nesting dolls I saw on the table, the ones that fit inside each other. I don't know which one is the real me."

"Most people have dreaming and reality all mixed up anyway," Kána said. "And it's not as important to distinguish between them as you would think. Or, at least, not in the *way* you would think."

Annalise nodded. As she looked around the room, she noticed, for the first time, the elaborate, web-like carvings on the petroglyph, and she remembered that Kána had mentioned them before. When Kána had explained the importance of the rock, Annalise had been in such a sleepy haze that she hadn't really looked at the carvings themselves. She'd just assumed they told stories in a language she couldn't understand.

But, now, as she studied how the strands of web linked together with such intricacy and complexity that no beginning or ending could be seen, she realized that the whole surface of the rock—top, bottom and sides—had been carved into a never-ending web. She began to feel like she could understand the rock, as if it spoke a universal language. She felt transfixed by the strands, and, as she examined them, they made her think of the many hallways she'd traversed on her recent journey.

Kána's eyes followed Annalise's as though following a thread of light and rested on the rock where Annalise's attention remained.

"The web offers many choices, Annalise." Kána said. "Everything is connected through the fabric of the universe."

Annalise's eyes widened. "Everywhere?"

"No. Every*thing*," Kána said. "Not just places, but times, people, plants, and stars, too; anything you can imagine, and even some things you cannot yet imagine."

Kána set the cloth down and placed her hand on Annalise's.

"Energy never dies," she said, looking toward the other couch, where Mabel and Mimi slept and snored and talked in their sleep. Following Kána's gaze, Annalise noticed something else she hadn't noticed before: that Mabel and Mimi looked a lot like Bob. Not that they resembled human men, of course, but, rather, that they appeared to be made of light and light only.

Annalise then looked down at her own arm and saw the same bright light that seemed to constitute Bob and the sheep. Kána's hand, on top of her own, also glowed, but inside Kána's glow dwelt the dense matter of flesh and bone.

Annalise continued looking around the room and saw that every physical thing had a glow emanating from it. She knew now that it had always been there but that she had just never noticed it before. What's more, she realized that even though she hadn't noticed it in the past, she could now see it in the eye of her memory. Ima, the waterfalls and rainbows, P.T. Skyler, the instruments on Acoustic Island, they had all been glow. But these Native Americans and their pueblo, the hospital, and the nesting dolls spread across the table, they were glow *and* matter.

"How curious," she said. "I always saw it, even when I didn't know I was seeing it."

She was reminded of a time years before when she was walking back from her cousin's house one late December evening. Her curfew was to come home before dark, but she'd barely made it that time. Christmas lights had already begun to twinkle on rooftops as dusk drew its curtains across the neighborhood. Through the windows, Annalise could hear chattering families gathering for their evening meals.

"Oh, I must hurry," Annalise had told herself, picking up the pace a bit until she was skipping, and even almost jogging, her way home. The nearer she'd gotten to her house, the more relieved she'd felt, until, finally, she was almost home. Then, even as much of a hurry as she'd been in, she saw something that stopped her right in her tracks. It was the next-door neighbor's house. They had turned their Christmas lights on, and when Annalise saw them, she realized that they had always been there, all year long, and even other years besides. They just hadn't been turned on except in December.

The thing that really got Annalise was that she realized she'd known all along that the lights were there; she just hadn't acknowledged it to herself. "I know things I don't know I know," she'd said. "*Wow!* I know things I don't know I know." Which, of course, turned into a song:

I know things
I don't know
I know
La la la

I know things
I don't know
I know
Tee hee hee
I know things I know
And I know things I don't
And I know all the things
That can be
La la la

Well, needless to say, Annalise's mom, although intrigued and impressed by Annalise's deep thoughts, took a more practical approach to the matter on account of her concern for Annalise's safety. She demonstrated this concern by giving Annalise the rest of the evening in her room alone to ponder the matter of what one knows, and what one doesn't, and what one *should* know, like to come home before it gets dark outside and your mother has worried herself sick.

"Well, why has my mind gone that way?" Annalise thought, wondering why she would think for so long about something as silly as Christmas lights when she had an entire glowing room around her.

Then, like a light bulb turning on, she saw the parallel, and, surprisingly, it wasn't the part about the light itself; it was the *always having been there* part. The only difference was that no one had turned this glow on the way they had the Christmas lights. This glow was always there, always had been, and always would be. Annalise just hadn't paid any mind to it in the past.

"Why didn't I notice before?" Annalise asked Kána while continuing to look around the room.

Yep, it glowed. She was sure of it. Tony glowed, and so did Kána, the table, the petroglyph, the dancers—everything.

Kána turned and said something to Tony in their language, and, when she did, Annalise saw a strand of light extend between them.

Suddenly, just as the light had seemed to flip from off to on, so now did color. Kána's glow, Annalise realized, was green, and Tony's was a soft blue. The strand between them was greenish blue, greener the closer it was to Kána, and bluer at Tony's end.

Tony walked over to the petroglyph and sat on it, his hands on his knees, his feet on the ground, and his eyes closed. His color changed from blue to violet and took on more of a wavering quality.

"The colors don't stay the same?" Annalise asked.

"Wonderful! You can see the colors already?"

"Yes. Tony's light just turned the most beautiful shade of violet."

"That's because he's connecting to his inner wisdom," Kána said.

"So violet means inner wisdom?"

"No," Kána replied. *"Tony's* violet *right now* indicates a connection with inner wisdom. I'm sorry to say there are no rules, Annalise. Unfortunately, you just have to learn through experience how to read the colors on your own."

She smiled gently at Annalise, who looked utterly perplexed.

"I know this is a lot to take in all at once," she said. "You've been through so much in a very short period of time. But try, if you can, to think of the act of smiling. Can you tell me a reason why you might smile?"

This seemed a strange question to Annalise, but she answered it anyway.

"Okay," she said after a minute. "Sometimes I smile because I'm happy."

"Good," Kána replied. "And can you think of another reason you might smile?"

"Well, sometimes when I'm embarrassed I smile just because I don't want anyone to know that I am embarrassed."

"Okay!" Kána said. "Now you're really thinking."

"And sometimes I smile just to be polite," Annalise said.

"Great," Kána replied. "You know, I don't smile when I'm embarrassed like you do. Instead, I turn red, and I have a tendency to look down at my feet. But I do smile when I don't know what to say. Do you do that, too?"

"Oh, no, I always have something to say," Annalise replied.

Kána laughed an open, easy laugh, the kind that says, "I'm laughing with you, not at you."

"Well. It's the same with the colors," she said. "The colors mean different things for different people and objects, and they change in relation to emotions, ideas, actions, interactions, situations, and so forth. You just have to interpret them as you go, just like you would a smile. Actually, it gets to where you don't even really have to think about it after awhile."

"Well, when you put it like that, I understand perfectly what you mean," Annalise said. "But I still don't understand why I can see the glowing colors now when I couldn't see them before."

Kána turned to look at Tony, and he nodded a single, consenting nod.

CHAPTER NINE

ANOTHER EYE

Mabel and Mimi stirred from slumber, and Annalise bounced exuberantly from the couch to the loveseat, plopping herself right between them. Kána, who'd been sitting on the hard, wooden coffee table to tend to Annalise, shifted to the more comfortable couch Annalise had been stretched out on, and Tony came over and sat quietly beside Kána. Annalise saw the strands of light that accompanied each movement, and she noticed, especially, the thick, strong strands connecting herself to Mabel and Mimi.

"I missed you guys while we were asleep!" she exclaimed, throwing her arms around their two necks with such force that she smashed them into an involuntary head butt.

"Wowie. That's a greeting," Mabel said.

"You can say that again!" Mimi said.

"Wowie. That's a greeting," Mabel repeated.

Mimi laughed heartily, even though the joke had made the rounds in their little world many times, and Kána, always generous with her laughter, chuckled also.

"I think you two get sillier every day," Annalise said, affectionately tousling the tops of their heads.

"Well, one thing is certain," Mimi said.

"What's that?"

"I'm awake now!"

"We're *all* awake now. And I'm ready to answer some long awaited questions," Kána said, scooting to the edge of the couch. Her skin emitted a multi-colored light that resembled a flame: blue in the center, orange at the edges. It was as if she were energy itself, come to warm up the room.

She quickly turned her head and shoulders toward Annalise and leaned forward in one swift motion, giving the impression that she might pitch herself into the plant on the coffee table in the process. Mabel, Mimi and Annalise drew in a collective, anticipatory breath.

"What first?" Kána asked, the fingers of her flame widening as though they would reach out and embrace Annalise, Mabel, and Mimi in their vigorous warmth.

"Breakfast," said Mimi.

"Yeah, I'm starved," said Mabel.

"You two *are* silly, aren't you?" Kána said. "You can ask anything you want, and all you can think of is food."

She patted her stomach and smiled to indicate that she understood about being hungry.

Mabel and Mimi, who prided themselves on their intelligence, glared at Kána. It was one thing when Annalise said they were silly, because they knew she meant it as a compliment, but with Kána they weren't so sure.

"Hmmmph," Mabel said.

"Well, I never," said Mimi. "You know we only eat greens, which are digested quickly. What on earth is silly about wanting them frequently? It seems logical to me."

Tony nodded.

"So you think you need to eat more often than us," he said. "But really you don't need to eat at all."

"It's hard to get used to," Mimi said.

"It is," Mabel agreed. "How about a little grass, at least? We don't need a fancy salad. Is there any grass here in the desert?"

Kána nodded, realizing the conversation wasn't going anywhere until the two sheep got fed.

Tony left the room and returned with a large blue plate covered with grass, which he placed on the coffee table in front of Mabel, Mimi, and Annalise.

"None for me, thanks," Annalise said, gesturing to the grass with a sweep of her hand and then smiling at Mabel and Mimi, who had already begun to munch. "But may I ask my question now?"

"Yes," Kána said. "I'm ready. Fire away."

"Well, why can I suddenly see all this light and color when I couldn't before?"

Kána and Tony looked at each other, and Annalise thought they had that proud look like parents get when their kid has just won a spelling bee or a field day competition.

"Annalise, this may sound a little fantastical to you," Kána said, "but when you traveled the way of the petroglyph, it opened up another eye, and now you see things as they really are, not just how they seem."

Annalise instinctively reached up and placed her hand on her forehead.

"My what?"

"You won't find it on your head," Kána replied. "It's in your mind. It's a new way of seeing things. This happened because your journey was successful."

"What journey? I didn't make a journey. All I did was fall asleep on the couch and have a strange dream about an eye and a bird and this weird place filled with hallways and a hurt kid and this mom who—"

"What was the first thing you said?" Tony asked, half-smiling.

"An eye," Annalise said, impatiently.

Tony's almost smile turned into an all-the-way smile, dissolving Annalise's impatience as it spread, until finally she just sat stupefied, with her mouth hanging open.

"Trying to catch a fly?" Tony asked warmly. "I thought you weren't hungry!"

Mabel and Mimi quit munching their grass and stared at Annalise, waiting for her to speak.

"Oh, my gosh," Annalise finally said. "I had a dream about an eye, and it was a passageway. It took me to—um—well, this is going to sound crazy, but, it took me to a room with a woman who was my mother, but not my mother."

"Yes, Annalise. You're right. She was your mother but not as you knew her before. She's been changed by grief."

"You mean that was really her? I want to help her. I want to go back right now."

Annalise jumped up from the couch and ran over to where Tony and Kána sat.

"Send me back," she said. "I know you can do it. Give me some more of that milk. Let me sit on the petroglyph. I want my mom."

"Annalise, sweetie, you have got to calm down," Kána said. "Your mom's going to be fine. She made it through your father's death, and she is going to make it through this, too. She's a very strong woman."

"But how did you know?"

"That your dad died when you were two?"

Annalise, who by now had sat down right on the coffee table in front of Kána and Tony, nodded her head.

"You could say, in a way, that your father is a friend of the tribe."

"Don't you mean my father *was* a friend of the tribe?" Annalise asked.

Kána shook her head.

"Remember how I told you energy never dies? Well, I guess you could say that whereas your father used to be a human *being*, he's now a human *been*."

At this statement, Tony busted out laughing. His broad shoulders shook ripples all the way down his poncho, shaking even the fringe at the bottom.

Kána shot him a stern look.

"I'm sorry," he said to Annalise. "But when Mom pops off with these things, I lose my manners."

"It's okay," Annalise said, and Tony saw from her face that it really was okay.

"Kids," Kána said, rolling her eyes at Tony. "My son's not trying to be rude, Annalise. Please understand. He knows your father's okay. He just forgot for a minute that *you* might not know it. Plus, he's got quite a sense of humor; that often comes with wisdom."

"Oh, I know about the humor from Bob," Annalise said. "I don't mind. But what can you tell me about my dad? How can I find him? And what about Mabel and Mimi eating the grass, and what about the washcloth on my forehead? Why do I need a washcloth on my forehead if I'm just a Light person now, like Bob?"

"Okay, okay, dear," Kána said kindly. "One thing at a time. First off, your dad. It's not up to us to give details, but I promise you'll meet again, when the time is right. That I know for sure. About the grass," she swept her hand toward the table, "Mabel and Mimi are transforming right now, and they still feel attached to their old ways. It's sort of like when a person loses an arm or leg in an automobile accident, but they still think it itches. Only in Mabel and Mimi's case, it's the whole body. Look at the plate of grass, and tell me what you see."

Annalise looked down at the big blue plate.

"It's almost empty now."

She could see from Kána's face that she hadn't given the answer Kána was looking for.

"What else?" Kána asked.

Annalise looked and looked at the grass, until finally she realized that it had no substance. It was just green light shaped like blades of grass. Same with the plate. The table, however, was both light and substance, like Kána and Tony. Apparently, Annalise still had some honing to do on her new skill.

"Light," Annalise responded. "Just light."

"Correct."

"And the washcloth?"

Kána nodded. "The same."

Annalise thought for a long, long time, like before when she tried to figure out what to do about the musicians on Acoustic Island. Kána and Tony, and Mabel and Mimi knew not to interrupt her, so they just let her think as long as she needed to.

Finally, after all that thinking, Annalise said, with utmost seriousness, to Kána, "Am I dead?"

Kána glided from the couch to the coffee table in a movement so swift and graceful that Annalise thought she'd imagined it. She draped her arm over Annalise's shoulders.

"Not exactly," she said.

"The girl in the bed?" Annalise asked.

"What would you like to know?"

"How do I get back to that room? Can I use the petroglyph again?"

"Of course you can, child, but it's not advisable. It wouldn't be permanent, and you would end up back here just like you did now. It's time to find your own way."

Annalise looked around the room as if it held some clue as to what, exactly, her own way might be.

Then she heard a voice. It was Me Anyou.

"Follow the silver cord," Me Anyou said.

Annalise walked around the whole room, examining every little thing. She saw the beautiful interplay of light and color, how each object, no matter how big or small, was its own world, complete and perfect just as it was. She saw how the dance of life, spinning and twirling around her, was an endless stream of possibilities, of untaken steps and moves. It was lovely. But, in all of this, she could not see, anywhere, a silver cord.

"I don't see it," Annalise thought.

"That's okay," Me Anyou thought back. "Your vision grows stronger and stronger. It will come."

"Yes, the chord is faint right now, very thin," Kána said, out loud, and Annalise realized that Kána could hear her mental conversation with Me Anyou. "It may take some time for you to rediscover."

Kána still sat with her hand on Annalise's shoulder, and, with her other hand, she reached into her pocket and produced a large, ornate key.

"I have something you may find helpful."

Kána pressed the key into Annalise's hand and then leaned over and kissed Annalise's forehead.

Tony came closer and kissed her forehead also.

"Many blessings, dear child," he said. "We will see you in another life."

"But I wanted to—"

"We know," Kána said. "We know. You are very welcome."

And then, without any further ado, Kána, Tony, the room, and the entire pueblo vanished as quickly as a coin in a magician's palm.

CHAPTER TEN

INTERROGATION

"Got yerself a key, did ya?" came the screeching voice. "Well, let's see it then."

Hagski held her palm up in the "give it here" gesture. She tap, tap, tapped her boot-clad foot on a cloud, which resonated like a big, hollow drum. She was dressed in some sort of uniform, but Annalise, not familiar with such things, couldn't identify it.

"Give it over, chickadee dee dee dee. No trying to weasel out of it, either, you little slippery slope, you little camel's nose, you little thin edge of the wedge."

Hagski bobbed her head side to side with attitude as she spoke.

"There's only one option here, Missy: An Official Examination; i.e., Hagski must examine all items of uncertain origin so they can be properly labeled, dated, stamped, recorded, re-packaged, sealed, confiscated, discarded, filed away, and otherwise processed."

She snapped her fingers, and a massive service counter sprung up right between the two of them, swallowing Hagski behind its tall blue and grey speckled facade. Directly in front of Annalise, the customer service window gaped like a wide, open mouth, waiting for food.

"Just a minute, please," Hagski called from some unseen spot behind the counter. She sounded as though she'd just realized someone was there.

Mabel and Mimi rolled their eyes at each other and turned toward a row of institutional looking plastic chairs, which had also appeared out of nowhere.

"This could take awhile," Mabel said.

"Indeed," said Mimi as they wove through ropes and posts toward the hard, cold chairs.

Annalise heard, emanating from behind the counter, a lot of rummaging, clanging, banging, fumbling and shifting around, and even a little bit of muttering and grumbling. There were, for instance, some "dad gummits" and two or three "gurshdarnits" floating about. It sounded like someone was digging through a big box full of pots and pans, or as if about fifteen toddlers had been set loose in a toy store with only one persnickety old woman to look after them.

Annalise heard one last loud crash, and then the noise died away, followed by the sound of approaching feet pattering on clouds. It seemed that Hagski had found what she was looking for. Drum, drum, drum came the pattering, nearer and nearer until the feet stopped just short of the service window.

"Ring the bell for service, please," Hagski said in a professional sounding voice. She still was not visible.

Annalise didn't see a bell, so she stood up on her tip-toes and looked left, all the way down the length of the seemingly endless countertop. There appeared to be no vanishing point, just blue and grey speckles as far as the eye could see. There was no bell, either, so she turned her head and looked to her right. Again, she saw nothing but blue and grey from here to forever.

Music began to play over the intercom system, and Annalise recognized the beautiful, haunting melody of a song she'd learned for music class right before the flood had carried her to the land of the clouds. She'd sung the song over and over to Mabel and Mimi while memorizing the lyrics.

"Under Your Nose" Annalise said.

"Why, yes," Mabel called from her chair. "By Pale Saint."

And together Mabel, Mimi and Annalise sang:

> Paint dries and feelings die
>
> What you wanted was always
>
> Under your nose

"That's it!" Annalise exclaimed, looking straight down for the first time since being asked to ring the bell. Sure enough, right beneath her very nose sat a silver bell. It was not the kind she expected to see, the kind where you just tap the top with your fingers to ding, like at the post office. Instead, it looked Christmassy, as if it had fallen right from Rudolf's reins and landed on the countertop. It was attached to an emerald green felt bow.

"You mean this jingle bell?" she asked.

There was no answer. The rummaging, clanging, banging, fumbling and shifting around started back up again.

"Pardon me," Annalise said a little louder this time. "Do you mean this jingle bell?"

A hand appeared from the hollow of the service window and placed a very official looking sign on the counter. The sign said, in large, blocky letters: PLEASE RING BELL FOR SERVICE. ANY PERSONS REFUSING TO RING BELL WILL, LIKEWISE, BE REFUSED SERVICE. HA.

Annalise lifted the felt bow from the countertop and jingled the bell. The ring sounded at an unusually high pitch and lasted such an inordinately, unnaturally long time that Annalise began to fear that the sound had lodged itself inside her ear and would never leave. When the shrill chiming finally did stop, she took great pains to set the bell down without ringing it again.

Hagski's face appeared in the service window.

"Why hello, Miss," she said, in a pleasant, cordial manner, as if she had just been waiting for someone to come along. "How may I be of service?"

"Oh, well, really I just need to know where to go next,"

Annalise said. "Is Bob around?"

"Bob," Hagski screeched, going from pleasant to perturbed in about one second flat. "What do I look like? A secretary? A message taker? A tour guide? How should I know where Bob is? Am I my brother's keeper?"

She broke eye contact and fiddled with the golden wings pinned to the lapel of her uniform. She seemed oddly vulnerable, even childlike, as she fiddled, and so Annalise began to feel badly for having upset her.

"Oh, well, I do beg your pardon," Annalise said, a little embarrassed. "I certainly didn't mean to offend you."

"Fine, then, but *you are going to have to answer some questions* now, little Missy. Or you're never going to make it past the security guards with that key."

Hagski disappeared behind the counter again, and, when she reappeared, she placed a clipboard, a stack of forms, a stamper, a labeling machine, a small box, a roll of packaging tape, and some bubble wrap on the counter, lining the items in a perfect row, with the exact same amount of space between each item. She then picked up the clipboard and a form from the top of the stack. She grabbed a pen from underneath the counter.

"Did you at any time leave this key unattended, even just for one minute to go and use the restroom or get a drink from the water fountain?"

"Well, actually, I only just got the key right before I came here."

"Quit trying to evade. Answer the question."

"Well, um, I really—"

"Answer."

"No."

Hagski tapped her long, square, manicured nail on the countertop. It was fancy, but chipped, the hot pink polish wearing off at the edges and a rhinestone star glued right in the center.

"Okay, were you well acquainted with the person who gave

you the key?"

"You mean had I known her long?"

"What has length got to do with it?" Hagski shrieked. "What I need to know is this: did you know her well? Did you trust her? Would you trust her with your life? Would you be a character witness for her in a murder trial?"

Annalise thought about it for a minute and then replied, "I think so. She seemed to be an extremely honorable person."

"There is no thinking here, no maybe," Hagski replied. "This is life or death. Do you trust her? Can you say, with absolute certainty, that she had only good intentions for the use of this key?"

"Well, I can't say *for certain,* but I think I know as well as one person can about another."

"Fine. Subject refuses to answer question," Hagski said, checking a box on her form. "Are you happy now?"

Annalise started to respond, but Hagski kept on talking.

"Well, what kind of key is it? They will want to know."

She made a huge production out of shuffling through the forms, finding the one she wanted and clipping it to her clipboard.

"Donkey or piano key?"

"Neither."

Hagski checked two boxes on the form.

"Key lime pie, key wrench?"

"No."

Check, check.

"Florida Key?"

"What's a Florida Key?"

Hagski leaned so far through the service window that her feet uprooted and she nearly toppled over to the other side. She gave Annalise the evil eye. Then she said, "Oh, you're tricky. Don't think I don't have your number, Missy. I know exactly what you're up to."

Check.

"Car key?"

"I'm not sure about that one."

Hagski frowned with disapproval.

"Well, how in the world can you not be sure about the function of your *very own* key?"

"It's like I said earlier. I only just got the key right before I came here."

"Are you trying to tell me you haven't even bothered to use it yet?"

Annalise nodded, and Hagski turned bright red with fury.

"You wasted all this time for nothing. Wasted forms. They'll have to be thrown away. Wasted ink. Wasted use of the clipboard. There will be fines. This kind of thing can't go unpunished. Then everyone would go around doing it. Oh, the chaos that would lead to!"

Hagski started to collect up the items she had set on the counter, and Annalise, feeling guilty, for she knew not what, offered to help.

"Absolutely not, you—you imbecile," Hagski spewed. "You'll just mess them up, get the papers out of order and such, you spotted toad, you mud caked toenail of a hog, you stinky cheese wedge on a stale bun, you five day old salami sitting on a countertop covered with ants, you pile of crusted over—"

"That's enough," Mabel said to Hagski.

"Yeah," Mimi said. "Can it, you old witch."

"Annalise, look what's happening," Mabel said, pointing a cloven hoof at the space between Annalise and Hagski. "Use what you learned at the Pueblo."

Annalise looked more closely at the space where Mabel pointed. The thread of light between Annalise and Hagski extended only from Annalise, she noticed. Around Hagski, instead of light, swirled a dark vortex that emanated nothing. It crackled as it consumed Annalise's light.

No wonder I feel so tired now, Annalise thought. Hagski does not share energy. She only takes it.

"You cannot have any more of my energy," she said to Hagski, turning her back on her.

The next destination, she now knew, would present itself with or without Bob.

All she had to do was make the leap.

"Come, dear friends," she said to Mabel and Mimi. "We have places to go."

CHAPTER ELEVEN
ANNALISE'S GARDEN

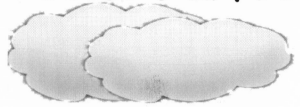

Annalise closed her eyes and leapt forward. She'd become as accustomed to cloud hopping as she'd once been to hopscotch, and, in just the same way, she'd begun to trust her leaps without having to look. But in the sky, of course, a fluffier, springier matter lay beneath her feet than at home, launching her not from concrete square to concrete square, but from cloud to cloud.

"Hot ziggity," Mabel exclaimed. "I could really get used to this!"

"Oh, me, too," Mimi said. "It's like …"

"It's like …"

"Absolute freedom," Mabel said, spinning also.

"Yes, like boundless possibility," Mimi added.

"No need to define it," Annalise said. "Let's just enjoy it."

With that, Annalise sprung from her cloud and somersaulted into the air, lingering midway a while before landing on the next cloud. Mabel and Mimi followed suit, each adding her own unique flair to her somersault.

"I feel like anything is possible," Mabel said.

"Like we could go anywhere or do anything," Mimi added.

"Well, let's go, then," Annalise said. "I see something interesting up there."

She pointed to a pathway of flat slate garden stones slightly overgrown with grass. Their different mixtures of gray, green, and brown blended perfectly with the grassy patches that surrounded them, creating almost a chameleon effect. Annalise hopped from her cloud to the nearest stone, and then to the next one, and then the next, and so on, until finally she and her two sheep stood before a large, arched, black iron gate. Embedded in the left door of the gate was the letter "A," and in the right door, the letter "H."

"Why, those are my initials!" Annalise exclaimed to Mabel and Mimi.

"Ah, so they are" said Mimi.

"Fabulous," said Mabel.

The three inched nearer the gate to get a better view of the elaborate iron that snaked and coiled to form Annalise's initials, but when they were nearly up to the gate, the doors swung open, revealing a familiar figure within. The man knelt among rows and rows of tomatoes, in the middlemost row, pulling weeds. He wore faded blue denim overalls with a bright yellow shirt underneath, and Annalise could see that as he pulled weeds he stuffed them into the abundant pockets of his overalls. Poking out of the pockets, between weeds and clumps of dirt, was a seemingly endless array of hand sized gardening tools that glistened in the sun.

"Bob!" Mimi and Mabel exclaimed.

Bob stood up and turned toward them, tipping his straw gardener's hat in greeting. As he did so, Annalise noticed, once again, the heart-shaped scar in the web between his thumb and index finger.

"What a delight!" he said. "You're early."

He headed toward them, and Annalise noticed that the bottoms of his overalls were rolled up, as if he had been wading in water and didn't want to get his pant legs wet. Dark, rich soil shook from the tops of his bare feet and into the lush green grass as he walked toward them.

Mabel and Mimi rushed to him, nearly knocking him over with the force of their hugs.

"Careful, ladies, careful. Mind the tools," he said, laughing and hugging them back. "Hugging is not supposed to be a contact sport, though with you three, I'm beginning to think anything is possible."

"We could say the same of you," Annalise said, running toward Bob with as little consideration for the tools as Mabel and Mimi had shown. "Besides, how can sheep made of light get injured by tools made of light?"

"Dear child," Bob said, beaming, "I see you've made progress. In fact, I expected to be fetching you before long, but here you are *ahead* of schedule, and on your own. I'm so proud of you for finding this place!"

"Thanks, Bob!" Annalise said, looking around. "But I don't think I've found it all the way yet. Where's the house?"

"House?"

"Yes, isn't this a magnificent estate or a glorious mansion of some sort?"

Bob laughed at Annalise's childish mistake of thinking that there had to be a house inside such gates.

"Oh, no, dear. This is a garden, a lavish, extraordinary garden with lawns and lawns of grass, and flowers, vines and shrubs, vegetables, herbs, fruit-bearing trees, nut trees, ponds full of fish, benches, swings, paths, and trails. It even has a labyrinth."

"A labyrinth?" Annalise asked, her eyes widening. "Can I see it?"

"Sure," Bob said. "But first let me take care of these weeds."

He turned around and walked into a central grassy spot where he removed clump after clump of weeds from his pockets. Finally he seemed to determine that his pockets were as clear of weeds as the rows of tomatoes he'd just tended.

"Feast your eyes on this," he said as he threw them up into the air, high above his head. They swirled and intermingled with the blues and whites of the sky.

"It's amazing," Mabel said.

"Oh, yes," said Mimi. "The weeds are spinning so fast they look like a perfect sphere."

"Not just any sphere," said Annalise, who was thinking of pictures she'd seen in science books at school. "It looks the way Earth does when you see pictures of it from space."

She turned to Bob, with a look of wonder.

"Bob," she said, "You made another Earth."

As soon as she spoke, the illusion vanished, and the weeds and soil quit spinning. They fanned out across the sky and fell rapidly to the ground, transforming into drops of rain just before hitting bottom.

"The lawn was thirsty," Bob explained casually, as if things like this happened every day.

"Is that what you always do with weeds?" Annalise asked.

"Yes, of course," Bob answered. "But that's not what they always do with themselves."

Annalise frowned and looked at Mabel and Mimi for help, but they just laughed.

"You should have expected an answer like that from Bob," Mabel said. "You know he speaks in riddles."

"Oh, of course you're right," Annalise said, lighting up again. "I get it, Bob. You mean you always throw them into the air, but they don't always become rain?"

"Precisely," Bob replied. "When they form the sphere, they become part of Mother Earth, and she decides what to do with them, which is to say that they decide what to do with themselves. They can become birds, flowers, air, grass, sunlight, deer, even weeds again."

Annalise's frown returned.

"If they might turn into weeds again, why do you bother to pull them?"

Bob chuckled.

"Someday you'll understand the irony of that question, but, for now, suffice it to say that pulling weeds will not always be necessary, as it is now. In fact, at some point there won't even be any weeds to pull."

"I just don't get it," Annalise said.

"No, of course you don't get it yet," Bob said. "If you did, there wouldn't be any weeds. I promise I will explain more later. But for right now, let's just enjoy each others' company and go see the labyrinth."

"Well, okay," Mabel said. "Let's do it."

"Right-o," said Mimi.

"Follow me, ladies," he said.

Annalise, Mabel, and Mimi fell in behind him, happily trotting along and asking questions about the various plants, flowers, and trees. At one point, Bob stopped to inspect a rose that had wilted a bit, and he held it in the upturned palm of his hand the way an adult might cup a child's chin. He spoke to it lovingly, with encouragement for growth and health.

"Just a wee bit of sunlight is all you need, dear heart," he said to the rose. "Just a wee bit of sunlight."

Annalise observed that as he spoke, sunlight radiated from the palm of his hand to the underside of the rose, setting the whole bush aglow with light. His own brightness intensified as he held the rose.

"How did you do that?" Annalise questioned immediately.

"With love," Bob answered, gently releasing the rose from his hand. "You can do it, too, if you want."

"But how do you have enough love for this whole, huge garden?" Annalise wondered, looking around in amazement.

"I think I know," Mabel said. "May I?"

"Go right ahead," Bob answered, pleased that Mabel had

spoken up.

"Love is infinite," Mabel said. "And whatever you use gets doubly replaced, so the more you use up, the more you have."

Bob nodded in agreement.

"Did anyone ever tell you you're smarter than your average sheep?" he asked, looking at Mabel affectionately as he turned away from the rose whose petals now spread into a sprightly, full-bodied, yellow bloom. Strands of yellow light shone from Bob onto Mabel as he spoke to her.

Mabel basked in it.

"And you, too, Mimi. You're a smarty, too," Bob added, now turning his brilliant warmth to Mimi. "Shall we continue?"

"Of course!" Mabel and Mimi said in unison. Bob, they later told Annalise, really knew the way to a sheep's heart.

Bob led them past a wide variety of plants and flowers in all sorts of colors, shapes and sizes, stopping sometimes along the way to help a forlorn bud or two. Each time he nurtured a plant, Annalise saw the light that passed from him to the plant and how the plant perked up once it received Bob's light.

Mabel and Mimi began to skip and sing, waving Annalise along until she joined in right between them, making her own merry lyrics to accompany theirs. But this time, something was different: the two sheep, who'd grown quite comfortable with their voices, sang more than just back-up, so that the verse resembled a sort of dialogue. And very soon a song was built which went something like this:

> In a beautiful garden
> a magnificent, beautiful garden
> La la la la
> La la la le
> Oh, yes – it's a beautiful garden
> la la la la
> la la la le

skipping along a flowered trail
la la la la
la la la le
with my two favorite sheep,
and our good friend Bob,
la la la la
la la la le
the Light man, Bob
the flower healer, Bob
la la la la
la la la le
and we're here with our dear
darling Annalise
la la la la
la la la le
in an enchanted, magical garden,
yes, a glorious, never-want-to-leave it garden
la la la la
la la la le
oh I love this place
oh we love this place too
la la la la
la la la le

"Bravo!" Bob said, motioning them toward the labyrinth. "That's the way to pass the time, ladies. The hike was a breeze with all that lovely singing."

"This maze is glorious," Annalise said, studying the sculptured, flowering bushes that formed the labyrinth. "Let's go inside!"

And she turned on her heel and began to march right toward the labyrinth with no hesitation whatsoever.

"Oh, wait a minute," Bob said, quickly catching her elbow. "I must correct you my dear, for this is not a maze, but a labyrinth, and while many perceive the two to be synonymous, a maze is a place to *lose* yourself, whereas a labyrinth is a place to *find* yourself. This is a critical difference that you must understand before you can enter."

"Oh, so when I thought I was in a maze of hallways at the hospital, I was really in a labyrinth of hallways?" Annalise asked, thinking of the body back in the hospital bed.

"Indeed," Bob said. "But this labyrinth will be very different from that one. And what you find inside will be different, too."

"Okay." Annalise said. "I can't wait. Let's go!"

"Right-o. Let's go," said Mabel, turning toward the labyrinth.

"I had no idea a bush could grow all the flowers," Mimi said. "Every kind of flower I've ever seen, right here, growing on the same bush."

"Yeah, in all the colors," Mabel said.

"And the smell," Mimi said, leaning in toward the labyrinth. "Why, I could just eat it."

"I know the smells and colors are enticing, ladies, but we must discuss a very important rule before anyone can enter."

"Oh, sure, Bob," Annalise said. "Of course."

"Okay," Bob said. "So here's the deal: Only one of us can enter at a time, because the labyrinth responds only to individuals, not groups. It literally forms a physical reflection of the problem your mind *most* needs to solve at any given time and actually reconfigures each time someone enters."

"But what if we, as a group, had a problem we needed to work out together?" Annalise asked.

"Well, now, that's an excellent question," Bob replied. "But, you see, the group still may only go in one at a time. Each person must figure out their own role in solving the problem. No two of us would play the exact same role, even in a group, so no two of us would experience the exact same labyrinth.

"Actually, no specific individual even experiences the exact same labyrinth twice, because each time you enter it you are in a different stage of your process, even if your mind is still working on the same problem."

Annalise backed up a bit and craned her head to look at the top of the labyrinth's entrance. It wavered like a mirage. From the center hung a wooden sign that read, "Home is Where the Heart Is." The entrance itself looked like two swans whose bent necks formed a heart.

"So the labyrinth is always becoming," Annalise said. It was half question, half statement.

"Yes," Bob said. "It reacts to the person who is closest to it. Watch this."

Bob stepped between Annalise and the labyrinth, and the labyrinth reacted with convulsive shaking, almost as if it had begun to cough. Leaves and flower petals fell off the shrubs, and then, just as suddenly as the convulsing had started, it stopped. The entrance closed up, and, off to the side, on a different wall, a new entrance formed in the shape of a lucky four leaf clover.

From the top of the new entrance dropped a metal sign that said, "Make Your Own Luck." And even as Bob stood there, the entrance changed to better reflect his shifting thoughts and feelings.

The sign changed to "Hope is a Many Feathered Thing," and then back to "Make Your Own Luck," and then to "A Pound of Pluck is Worth a Ton of Luck," and once more to "Make Your Own Luck."

"They're subtle changes," Bob said, noticing that Annalise watched the sign attentively. "But they reflect the configuration of the labyrinth within, which, of course, reflects the current state of my ever changing mind."

"It's all so exciting," Annalise said. "Bob, why don't you go first?"

"Oh, no, thanks, Annalise. I've gone many times already. You go ahead."

"Mabel, Mimi?" she asked, turning toward the sheep. Now that she knew they could only go in one at a time, she didn't want to be rude and rush in.

Mabel and Mimi shook their heads and gestured for Annalise to enter.

"Well, you don't have to tell *me* more than once," Annalise said, skipping toward the labyrinth, whose entrance now resembled a large, ornate key.

As Annalise entered, Bob, Mabel and Mimi saw the sign above her head change to read, "There is No Place Like Home."

"Anna, look up," shouted Mabel, who knew that the sign quoted one of Annalise's favorite books.

Annalise stopped beneath the sign, looked up, smiled, did a little twirl, curtsied to her friends, and, without any further ado, disappeared inside the labyrinth.

CHAPTER TWELVE

A LABYRINTHIAN TWIST

Inside the labyrinth, a strong, warm wind whipped around Annalise, lifting a swarm of leaves and flower petals into a swirl around her feet. The mass of debris pulled her forward as it twisted higher and higher, up around her whole body and past her head, where it lifted her hair into a dancing frenzy. Her mind was filled with questions for the labyrinth, problems for it to solve.

"Well, this labyrinth isn't so very hard," she said. "I don't even have to decide where to go. The wind just takes me along."

She stretched her arms out as far as she could reach on both sides, and the debris slapped against the palms of her hands, spinning her around like a pinwheel. Then she pulled her arms back into her body to stop the motion. Again and again she repeated this movement, spinning, then not spinning, then spinning again.

"It's just lovely in here," she said when she finally took a moment to study the flurry that surrounded her. "I wonder if all tornadoes are this beautiful inside."

And then, "Of course not, silly!" she replied to herself. "Most tornadoes are not made up of fluttering flower petals."

For a minute she thought about what a shame that was, but this last thought she did not speak out loud because she'd started to listen to something other than the ideas rumbling around inside her own head. All of a sudden, layers upon layers of voices had begun to whisper to her simultaneously, creating a clamorous distraction. It was like hearing people sing in rounds; only instead of singing they were, of course, whispering. And every one of them said something different.

At first she only caught a word or two here or there, but eventually she could hear and understand entire phrases. It sounded something like this:

"... good when you helped the teacher."

"Making up songs in the valley ..."

"... trying so hard to find your mom."

"... on the island with your sheep."

"You thought it was some other ..."

"... the dream about cats circling the oak."

And that's how they spoke, not one voice after another, but one voice *while* another. The very bushes whispered to her about her life: places she'd been, people she'd known, conversations and dreams she'd had, decisions she'd had to make.

"I know you," the labyrinth proclaimed. "I understand you. I can help you."

Soon it wasn't merely the leaves that swirled around Annalise but, rather, the whole labyrinth that spun, for when she started listening she stopped walking, and when she stopped walking, the labyrinth started spinning around her, rotating her deeper and deeper into its core.

The whispers came more and more at a time until the overlap created a fabric that told Annalise's life story. Each flower, each leaf of the bush had a part of Annalise's tale to weave, and each in its own voice, with its own emphasis. Annalise heard themes emerging from the different voices. One was concerned with faith and hope, and another complimented Annalise's creativity and wisdom. They spoke about courage, suffering, and joy. They praised her modesty and kindness but pointed out times when she'd been jealous or greedy.

Then, as suddenly as it had started, the spinning stopped, and the debris fell to the ground with a final swish. Annalise could now see beyond her own nose well enough to determine that she'd been spun into the central grassy area of the labyrinth, which was spherical and had many entrances—or exits, depending on which way you were going. Each of these entrances had a shimmering pathway comprised of swirling colors. It appeared as though the pathways were moving, but when Annalise looked closely, she realized that it was only the colors that were in motion. The pathways led to the heart of the labyrinth, where a table stood, and upon it sat an open book. At the beginning of the pathway closest to Annalise, a sign read, "Ask ONE question of the book, please."

"Well, that's a long pathway," Annalise said as she sight-measured the distance to the book. "The table is as far from the sign as my mailbox is from my house."

She tapped the pathway with her foot to see if she could determine what kind of material it was made of and discovered that it felt slippery and hard, like glass. The colors formed the shape of a splash around her foot, with the part nearest her foot and directly beneath it turning solid blue. When she lifted her foot, the colors returned to their original appearance. She bent down and ran her hand over the smooth surface in a wavelike motion and watched how the area directly beneath it became solid pink, with streaks of pink trailing behind.

"It's like a giant, magical sketch pad," Annalise said. "And I am the artist."

"It's true," the bushes said.

"Right you are."

"You are the artist."

"Tap that foot."

"Thank you. Thank you. Thank you," Annalise said, and dipped them a curtsey.

"Such manners," they said.

"Better listen up."

"Such a polite girl."

"Heed the counsel."

"Assistance forthcoming."

The bushes began to give her advice. There was, apparently, a right way to walk the path and a wrong way. Because each and every step would reconfigure the pathway, she must, these voices said, walk with right intention and mindfulness in order to reach the book. And she must have the right effort and concentration.

"But how do I know what is right?"

"You know," the voices buzzed, and for once they all said the same thing, although not really at the same time.

"Well, if they all think I know, then I must know," Annalise thought, and she kicked both of her shoes off and stepped one foot and then the other onto the iridescent trail, very cautiously, so as to not slip. Once she'd firmly placed both her feet on the pathway, her thoughts shifted. She quit focusing on all the answers she wanted to get from the labyrinth, and even temporarily let go of her fierce desire to return home and see her mother. Instead, she just concentrated on walking the pathway.

She noticed pink, yellow, and orange lights coming from the table and the book. The light shooting off looked like a colorful sunrise.

The table itself, she now realized, had only one central leg or stem, and that stem resembled a totem pole, though it was, of course, not as tall. The most striking difference between this stem and a regular totem pole was that symbols, rather than faces, were carved up and down the length of it. Some of the symbols Annalise knew, and some she did not. The cross, for instance, she recognized, and also a crescent moon with a little star in the hollowed out part. There was a triangle with an eye in it, a wheel that looked like a captain's wheel, a star that was made out of two triangles, a circle that looked like it had one black whale and one white whale in it—she thought she'd heard her mother call this one yin yang, but she wasn't sure—and many, many more.

As Annalise examined the glowing pole, the many leafed voices of the bushes died down, and a single voice came from the direction of the book.

"Welcome," it said.

Now, of course, with all the glowing going on, it's easy to guess who Annalise thought was there.

"Bob?" she asked.

"No."

"But your voice, it's so familiar. I know you."

"It's Me," the voice said. "Me Anyou. Have you thought of your question?"

"Why are you in a book?"

"Am I?"

"Well, I don't know. That's why I'm asking."

"Is that your one question?" Me Anyou asked, laughing kindly.

"Oh, no, no," Annalise said. "Certainly not."

"My turn to ask, then," Me Anyou said.

"Okay," Annalise replied. That seemed fair enough to her. A question for a question.

"Do you remember what Bob told you about me?" Me Anyou asked.

"He only said that he was one manifestation of Me Anyou, one of millions."

"That is correct," Me Anyou said. "So then what can you surmise about the book?"

"That you are, I mean *it is*, another manifestation of Me Anyou?"

"Precisely."

"Well, why are you glowing so much, and why are you three different colors? You look like a beautiful sunrise."

"Why, thank you. Is *that* your question?" Me Anyou asked.

"Well, no. That's not a big enough question for my one and only."

"And besides, it's really two questions anyway," Me Anyou said, laughing again. "You are a curious girl, and that's good. But let me ask you something now."

"Okay," Annalise said, a little tentatively. Maybe this wasn't fair after all, she thought. Me Anyou wasn't answering her questions but kept asking more. Yet it occurred to her that her replies to Me Anyou were somehow answering her own questions. Maybe Me Anyou was just teaching her to ask the right things.

She had an idea.

"I know how to figure out my one question," she said. "That is, when you're done with yours."

The glow surrounding the book expanded and contracted a few times, as if it were breathing.

"Well, if you know how to figure out what you want to ask," the voice said, "then there is no more need for my inquiries."

"Great!" Annalise said. "That's what I thought you'd say."

"What is your question?" Me Anyou asked.

"I'm not quite sure yet, but I've learned from you that I already have the answers if I can just figure out the right questions. And since the questions are all answers to other questions, I must know them, too, since they are answers."

"*Now* you're thinking," Me Anyou replied. "You may proceed."

Annalise closed her eyes and thought really hard. "Self, my question is, 'What is my question?'"

A gentle wind frolicked through the grass, bending blades to and fro in a dazzling spectacle of green. Annalise, who'd opened her eyes for just a minute, drank in this sight before closing them again. She felt the warm, soft wind on her face, the sun streaming in from the top of the labyrinth, the cool, hard surface of the path beneath her feet, and she was suddenly overcome with love for it all.

"I love this world!" she declared, thinking not only of the world inside the labyrinth and the garden, but of the world back home, too.

Perhaps the glistening green had triggered her emotion; or was it the influence of the labyrinth that impassioned her so? Whatever the cause, the result was certain, for suddenly she knew her question, clear as the day that unfolded its own unique design around her.

She began walking forward, approaching the book with ease. With each step she took, she felt the energy of the trail surge into her body through her bare feet. She now understood why Bob had taken his shoes off, and she had an impulse to walk barefooted everywhere she had ever been and everywhere she would ever go. She imagined sand, grass, silt, carpet between her toes and felt a deep, deep connection to the earth and her own special path upon it.

"How can I best contribute?" she asked, now just steps away from the book. "What can I do to help other people? How can I make the world a better place?"

And though it may seem that Annalise asked several questions, in reality, it was just one question that she asked, rephrased in different ways. For, everything had now begun to make sense: the webs she had seen, Me Anyou and every manifestation of Me Anyou, the strands of light between people and objects. It was all clear now. Each decision, each action, no matter how big or small, affected everything else.

Annalise, who was now close enough to touch the book, reached down and closed it so that she could read the title. Upon the deep green cover were gilded, decorative letters that read: *The Marvelous Life of Annalise Alexia Humphrey: A History and Guide*. But instead of saying "Written by" the way a normal book did, it said, "Manifesting by Annalise Alexia Humphrey." Beneath the writing was an illustration of a golden pen dipped into a golden pool of ink, and in that pool of ink was a reflection of Annalise's face, exactly as it looked at the present moment.

Me Anyou spoke. "Annalise, dear, because you asked the question you were meant to ask, you now have access to all the answers. Whenever you need this book, you'll be able to summon it to your mind's eye. Of course, I have to warn you, the book changes according to your thoughts and actions. That's why there is a birth date but no death date, and, of course, this is the reason that much of the book is still blank."

Annalise opened the book and began to flip through the pages. It was all there: her father's death, the journeys with her sheep, her body being carried away by the flood, good and poor choices she had made so far in her short life, footnotes on how to make better decisions in the future, negative personality traits and beliefs—which, she now understood, were like weeds and needed removal. She saw that the last complete chapter dealt with making choices and that each choice had a forking path with outcomes. She saw that from the prongs of these forks were more decisions and more forks and more forks and more and more and more into infinity, literally running off the page.

"It's best not to look too far into the future, since it's changing anyway," Me Anyou said. "As you make decisions, you will see that they become part of the history section, and forks that were not previously visible on the pages of the choices chapter will become visible a little bit at a time."

"This is amazing," Annalise said. "How can I ever thank you?"

"Just keep asking the same question," Me Anyou answered. "But there is one thing you need to understand about this book, Annalise."

"What is that?"

"It doesn't exist in isolation. It's connected to millions and millions of other books, some, of course, more closely than others.

What happens in those books impacts your book, and what happens in your book impacts those books."

Annalise then noticed that the streams of light which she had compared to a sunrise were actually clusters of threads connecting her book to other books. The books were everywhere: on the ground, in the bushes, floating in the air; many of the strands even continued on beyond Annalise's field of vision.

Annalise stood for a minute, taking it all in, remembering it for her mind's eye. It was so beautiful and so serene that she wished she could stand there forever, but she did want to get back to her mom, and she also wanted to give the sheep a chance to experience the labyrinth.

"Thank you," she said, finally. "I will always, always remember this moment." And she turned to walk back down the path in the direction from which she had come.

Then, when she was about midway through the path, something began to move inside her pocket, almost like it was dancing or trying to get out. "I must have a jumping bean inside my pocket," she said.

Then she remembered the key.

When she got back to the beginning of the iridescent pathway, she stopped and pulled the key out of her pocket and, for the first time, really examined it. The top of the key, the part that you hold to turn, resembled a cute little monkey with a bright red hat on its head. Its ridged tail was the key itself.

"Well, aren't you just adorable?" Annalise said to the key. And, before she knew what had happened, the monkey leapt from her hand, pounced on the ground and hopped to the outer part of the labyrinth.

Annalise, of course, followed after the monkey.

CHAPTER THIRTEEN

OUT TO PASTURE

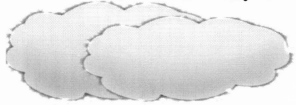

"**O**hmygosh! Mabel, Mimi, Bob!" Annalise exclaimed, running out of the labyrinth toward her three friends. "That labyrinth is the best. You just have to go in."

She skipped over and planted a kiss on Bob's cheek.

"I take it you found your answer?" Bob asked, receiving the kiss.

"Oh, yes, and many, many more. In fact, I found all the answers," Annalise said, twirling around with glee.

"All the answers?" Bob asked, tilting his head to make eye contact with the spinning girl. "How is that possible?"

"Well, I found a path to all the answers I need for me," Annalise clarified.

"Ah, now that makes sense."

"Who's next? Who wants to go now?" Annalise asked, jumping up and down and clapping.

"Um, that might be a bit of a problem," Mabel said, pointing a hoof in the direction of the labyrinth. Only, technically, it was not so much *in the direction of the labyrinth* as it was *where the labyrinth used to be*.

Annalise turned and caught the very uppermost tip of hedge sinking into the ground as if being swallowed by quicksand.

"What the heck—I mean where—I mean *what* is going on?"

Annalise exclaimed, watching the labyrinth disappear before her eyes.

"Ah, yes, *that*," Bob said. "Apparently you no longer have need of the labyrinth."

"Me? But what about the others?"

"Mabel and Mimi have their own garden," Bob replied. "This one is yours."

"But, I don't understand."

"This garden—and everything in it—is the product of your mind, Annalise. It's the harvest of your thoughts, emotions, and actions, a reflection of your life, much like the book you saw in the labyrinth, or the labyrinth itself."

"But if it's a reflection of *my* life, how did you go in the labyrinth before, and how are you, Mabel, and Mimi here in my garden right now?"

"Just because you created it doesn't mean you're the only one who can visit."

"So when we first got here and you were pulling weeds, that means *you* come here to tend *my* garden?" Annalise asked Bob.

"Yes."

"But why?"

"I'm your guide," Bob said. "I want to do this for you."

"Aw, thanks Bob," Annalise said, throwing her arms around his neck. "You know what, though? I don't think there'll be as many weeds from now on."

"Nor do I," Bob said. "I'm very proud of you. And now I'll be able to mainly relax when I come here."

"Well, I sure do wish Mabel and Mimi could have gone in that amazing labyrinth," Annalise said. And, as she said it, the barest tip of hedge began to rise back out of the ground.

"Oh, no, no, Annalise. Don't you worry about that," Mimi said. "If we want to go in labyrinths, they'll be in our own garden."

"Are you sure?" Annalise asked.

Mabel and Mimi nodded, and the hedge began to sink back down.

Bob now looked at Mabel and Mimi. "Girls," he said, "I have some important news. You may not like it at first, but soon you'll understand that it's what needs to happen."

Mabel and Mimi didn't look surprised at all, but Annalise was alarmed, and turned away from the sinking hedge to face Bob fully.

"What is it?" she asked.

"I'm afraid it's time for the three of you to part ways."

"Part ways? I don't understand." Annalise moved closer to Mabel and Mimi and put her arms around their necks.

"Don't worry, you'll always be able to find each other. You just won't be travelling the same path anymore."

"But why? I don't understand. Tony said they were my totems. They're my best friends."

"Now, now," Mimi said, patting Annalise on the shoulder with her hoof. "Don't you worry about us. We're going to our own garden to stay for a while, and you can continue on your journey."

"But I don't want to leave. I want to see your garden. Will you be together? Where is it? How will I find you? How will you find me?"

"Come now," Bob said. "Let's go see, shall we?" And he lifted a foot and stepped onto a translucent stair that appeared from nowhere and seemed to be made of the same fabric as the blue sky that surrounded it. Annalise, Mabel, and Mimi watched as stair after stair appeared beneath Bob's feet to support his ascent into the clouds.

"Come on," he said, stopping mid-cloud and waving them up. What a vision he was: a Light man climbing up the sky on transparent stairs.

Mabel and Mimi giggled at the sight of it.

"Well, okay," Annalise said. "If they do have to stay, I certainly want to make sure their garden is nice." She stepped onto the stairway that formed in Bob's wake.

"Is this the only way to get there?" Mabel asked, stepping up behind Annalise.

"I wondered when someone would ask that question," Bob shouted down. "No, it's not the only way. It's not even the easiest way, but it works best for us right now. You'll find your own ways in time."

Annalise watched as Bob disappeared into the clouds, and then, following behind him, she climbed on through the layers of white puff herself. Everywhere around her was suddenly green, green, green, as far as the eye could see, and it reminded her of the Verdant Hills, except that here the sun shone brilliantly, whereas in the Verdant Hills she mainly remembered rain and clouds.

"This is the most beautiful pasture I've ever seen," she said to Bob.

"Glorious, isn't it?"

"Oh, yes, indeed," Annalise said as she continued to scan the landscape, noting the lush, vibrant patches of clover that punctuated the rolling hills. The hills went on, it seemed, as far as the eye could see, and Annalise noticed that nestled in the valleys between these hills, bubbling streams wended to and fro, over rock and stone, converging at various points and then forking back off again.

Atop one of the hills, not too far in the distance, an old fashioned red barn was filled to bursting with hay and lined with troughs of sparkling, clean water. Next to this barn were rows and rows of all kinds of lettuce, a treat of which the sheep had grown quite fond. Here and there, randomly scattered, over both hill and valley, were great, wide shade trees beneath which could have fit entire flocks of sheep.

"Oh, I think you two are going to like it up here," Annalise shouted down to Mabel and Mimi, who'd been slowed down by climbing the stairs on hooves.

"It's amazing," Mimi said, breaking through the clouds and stepping onto the pasture that now lay beneath her hooves.

"Stunning," said Mabel.

The two sheep looked at each other and smiled deep, appreciative smiles.

"Who is that?" Mabel then asked, pointing to a robed Light person sitting underneath a tree.

The person stood and waved at Bob, and Bob waved back.

"There are many names," Bob said. "The Good Shepherd, The Enlightened One, The Light Giving Lamp, The Blessed Virgin, Tara, Krishna—" he trailed off in a way which indicated that it would exhaust him to name them all. Then he said, "There are many forms, and many names."

"Is that a man or a woman?" Annalise asked. "I just can't tell from the names."

"Depends on the chosen form," Bob responded. "But I have a feeling these sheep have an affinity for shepherds, so this prophet will most likely be male."

Then, as if on cue, the robed being under the tree leaned over and picked up a staff that Annalise had not noticed lying in the grass beside him. He began to make his way toward them, and Annalise saw that his long brown hair hung past his shoulders in matted clumps.

"Does he ever brush his hair?" she asked Bob. "My mom would kill me if I let mine get like that."

"That style he wears, I think the young people call it dreadlocks."

"You mean he does it on purpose?"

"You'll get used to it."

As the shepherd approached, he smiled at Mabel and Mimi. His kind eyes invited them to come to him, and when he was just a few feet away he stopped and opened his arms, allowing the sheep to rush into the folds of his robe. He circled his arms around them, and they nuzzled and burrowed up to his chest. Annalise thought that she had never seen them so look so contented.

"Is Me Anyou here, too?" Annalise asked Bob.

"Child, don't you know by now that Me Anyou is everywhere? This shepherd is not only a manifestation of Me Anyou, but a *perfect* manifestation of Me Anyou, and he always, always acts in accordance with Me Anyou's wishes. Didn't you see Me Anyou by the tree over there a few minutes ago when the shepherd was meditating?"

"Oh, you mean when the shepherd was connecting to his inner wisdom?" Annalise asked.

"Is that how Kána explained meditation to you? She's a smart lady."

"Yes, and my mom meditates, too. I just understand it better now that—"

Annalise slapped her hand to her forehead and stopped mid-sentence.

"Oh, my gosh," she said. "Talking about Kána reminded me. I've lost something very important. There was a key, I mean a *mon*key. I followed it out of the labyrinth, and then, well, I found out about Mabel and Mimi, and I came here. Oh, no. I can't believe I forgot the monkey. I meant to—"

"It's okay, Annalise. It's okay. Check your pocket."

"But you don't understand. It got really big, and it was hopping around, and—"

"Just go ahead and check your pocket," Bob said, with a mischievous look in his eye.

"Well, what the heck," Annalise said. Bob had never led her astray before. And after all he had done for her, she could, at the very least, humor him and check her pocket. Then maybe he would listen and they could go find the monkey.

She stuck her hand in her pocket, with an irritated

"hmmmmph," and to her amazement, a furry little monkey jumped on the top of her hand, ran up her forearm, paused for a second of confusion at the elbow, turned ever so slightly to follow the crook, and then ran the rest of the way up her arm and perched itself smugly on her shoulder.

CHAPTER FOURTEEN

MONKEY'S UNCLE

Saying goodbye to Mabel and Mimi was not easy but would have been much worse if Annalise hadn't been able to see how happy they were in their new pasture.

"There's one thing I don't understand," she said to Bob. "I mean, how come I have my own garden but Mabel and Mimi share one?"

"Noticed that did you? Well, sheep are very special creatures," Bob replied. "The word 'sheep,' I'm sure you've noticed, is both singular and plural?"

"Yes."

Bob stepped back over to the clouds and began his descent on the stairway.

"Well?" Annalise asked.

"Well what?"

"The sheep? Plural and singular?"

"Oh. That's it."

"That's it? What do you mean that's it?"

"You're a smart girl. You can figure it out."

"Well, okay then. I'll just have to think about it," Annalise said, patting the monkey that now clung to the top of her head like some kind of crazy, misshapen fur hat.

"You and me," the monkey sang.

"You and me, sitting in a tree, e-a-t-t-i-n-g, first a banana, then a coconuta, then we get a knife and smear on some buttah."

"You're supposed to spell 'eating' with one T," Annalise said to the monkey.

"T shmee, purple elephants run free," the monkey spat back at her, upon which a herd of purple elephants ran by, and Annalise had to jump out of the way quickly to avoid being stampeded.

"Four wallaby *tea*-totalers sipping beneath a tree," the monkey continued.

There appeared suddenly four tea drinking wallabies under one of the trees. They conversed as they drank, discussing the weather, and they politely passed biscuits, scones, and muffins to one another and dabbed the corners of their mouths with embroidered linen napkins. Then, poking his head out from his mother's pouch, one of the joeys caught sight of the purple elephants, squealed with glee, and began to hop after them. The other wallabies followed, knocking over the table and all of its contents.

"Oh, dear," said a mama wallaby, pausing for a second and then deciding that chasing after and protecting her joey was more important than cleaning up the mess.

"T-t-t-t-t-rex," the monkey said. "T-Rexosauras, ronossaurus, Tyrannosaurus Rex chasing a wallaby, chasing an elephant, running past Annalise and me."

"Oh, no," Annalise said as a T-Rex ran by.

"Oh, yes, yes, yes," said the monkey. "These and many more T things: swollen thumbs, bigger than tree trunks; roaring tigers; tee-time at the golf course; tanks with guns and torrents of wind; clucking turkeys riding tornadoes—"

"Stop!" Annalise screamed, amid the rapidly expanding chaos that surrounded her.

"What's the magic word?"

"Please?"

"Good start. Is there anything else you want to say to me?" the monkey asked.

"I don't know," Annalise said.

"Trickling tarantulas, trains off the tracks, turtles playing tambourines, typists at typewriters typing the letter T."

"Okay, okay, I get it. You can have as many T things as you want in your song. E-a-t-t-i-n-g. Is that how you want it? You've got it."

"Why, thank you, Annalise. How very decent of you," the monkey said, hopping from her head back down to her shoulder.

The chaos subsided, and Annalise looked into the distance where Mabel and Mimi sat talking with the shepherd inside a bubble of light. They were in their own world and hadn't noticed any of the mischief the monkey had caused.

"Bob," Annalise called down to the clouds.

No answer.

"Bob, the monkey's gone crazy. I need help."

Annalise began to descend the stairs back to her own garden, but when her head broke through the clouds, she saw that what she approached was not her garden at all, but, rather, another layer of clouds.

"I knew it," came the familiar screeching voice from somewhere within the clouds.

"You've got my monkey. Monkey see, monkey do. Monkey mind, monkey on your back. *Quit monkeying around!* I want my monkey, monkey, monkey," Hagski shrieked.

"Well, now, I thought that monkey reminded me of someone," Annalise said to herself. "It's just as crazy as Hagski is. But it's my key. Kána gave it to me."

"Kána didn't give you anything. You already had the monkey. You've always had it, but it's mine, and I want it back."

"You don't make any sense," Annalise said. "How could I have always had it if it was yours, and how come I saw Kána give it to me if it was already mine?"

"You doofus. You had the *mon*key, not the *key* key. She had to give you the key so that you'd know you had the monkey. You were monkey blind. Now you see it. But I've said too much already. Just hand over the monkey, become an ignoramus again, and be on your way, please. You'll grow a new monkey to replace that one, anyway."

The monkey clung to Annalise's head again. It screeched at Hagski and raised its fist and shook it in the air. Annalise wasn't sure if the gesture was meant for her or Hagski, but the screeching was clearly for both.

Annalise wanted nothing more at that moment than to be rid of the monkey, but she knew, somehow, that handing the monkey over to Hagski was not the right thing to do. What a nuisance the monkey was, interfering with where Annalise wanted to go, distracting her and causing commotion, misspelling words, screeching like a lunatic. She couldn't think two clear thoughts in a row with that monkey clinging to her head and raising a ruckus, but she knew Hagski, and she knew Kána, and she knew that if Kána wanted her to have the monkey, and Hagski did not want her to have the monkey, then she needed to keep the monkey, no matter how things appeared.

"I am *not* giving you this monkey," Annalise said to Hagski. "This is my monkey, and I will decide what to do with it."

Just then, as if to totally disprove Annalise's statement, the monkey leapt from her head to Hagski's head and began to shake its fist again.

Annalise held her hand out to try to coax the monkey back, and she even began to coo at the monkey, to no avail. The monkey continued its incessant, incoherent, shrieking chatter until finally Annalise couldn't take it anymore.

"Fine," she said. "Why don't you just go find a tree to live in or something? You little beast."

And, of course, as you might suspect, trees began popping up everywhere through the clouds, left and right, forward and backward, and the monkey leapt from tree to tree hurling bananas, coconuts, and various other fruits at Hagski and Annalise, who had quit arguing because they were busy dodging flying fruit.

"Come to Mama," Hagski said to the monkey when she'd regained her composure.

"No, no, no!" the monkey said, pouncing down from a tree and onto the top of a cloud where he proceeded to jump up and down like a child doing stunts on a trampoline. He did the splits ten or fifteen times in rapid succession, touching his toes at the highest part of the jump, then switched from the splits to pulling his knees into his chest. Next he added a little flip, which he did ten or fifteen times before bouncing onto his bottom and springing back up again. When he'd quit his flipping and bottom bouncing, he grabbed hold of his tail and lassoed it around his head like a cowboy. All this he did while sticking his tongue out at Hagski and Annalise.

Then, just when Hagski and Annalise thought the show was over, the monkey plopped onto a banana peel, as though he were hopping onto a sled, and aimed it down a tunnel which had extended suddenly from the clouds. The tunnel was angled like a slide and led down to who knows where. The monkey, undaunted, and even with great intention, grabbed hold of the top part of the tunnel, pulled his banana-sled back and forth a few times to gain momentum, and then gave a little shove off, disappearing into the dark, mysterious cavity.

"Wooohoooo," Annalise and Hagski heard echoing up from the tunnel. "Woooohooooo wooohoooo woooohoooooooooooooo. This is funnnnnnnnnnnnnn."

Annalise looked at Hagski and then down the tunnel and then back at Hagski again. She could see nothing in the tunnel, yet she could hear that the monkey's voice grew fainter as he got further away.

"Do you know where it goes?" Annalise asked.

"How should I know? It wasn't even here a minute ago," Hagski replied.

"Well, do you think he'll come back?"

"What do I look like, a zookeeper?" Hagski asked. "Do you think I'm a psychic? A primate specialist? A tunnel mapmaker? Your personal safari guide?"

Annalise could see that Hagski would be of no assistance whatsoever, so she decided that it was time to take the matter into her own hands.

"I must not give myself time to get scared," she said aloud. And then, without another word or thought, she jumped quickly down the tunnel after the monkey.

Hagski stood in stunned silence at the top of the tunnel, gaping after Annalise.

"Well, I'll be a monkey's uncle," she said.

There was no response from Annalise, who'd gotten too far away to hear her and now slid onward to an uncertain, uncharted destination.

CHAPTER FIFTEEN
PASSAGE TO YEHIDAH

With the rapid movement downward and the sudden darkness, Annalise's sight became blurry. The tunnel felt slick, like glass or ice, and a cold breeze wafted up from somewhere below.

"Bbbbbrrrrrr," Annalise said to herself as she shivered and chattered her teeth. "That monkey sure is lucky to have fur."

She folded her arms close to her body to try to get warm, but the compactness just accelerated the sliding, which, of course, created more breeze and only made her colder.

"I must get my mind off of this icy air," she said. "I'll just pretend I'm somewhere else."

She tried to envision palm trees and sand and sunshine, but soon discovered it was quite difficult to imagine tropical climates while hurtling down a bitter cold tunnel with nothing to look at.

"Well, I might as well forget that since it isn't going to work anyway," she said. And then she began to wonder how she would describe this sensation if she had to write a story about it for school.

"It feels like there's too much air on my skin," she thought. And again she wished she had fur, which made her then wonder where the monkey had gone.

"Monkey?" she called out.

"Monkey . . . monkey . . . monkey," the tunnel resounded with an eerie, hollow tone.

"Monkey, are you down there?" she repeated.

Still the only response was the echoing of her own voice.

"Well, I guess I'll think a little more about being cold."

"It feels like little needles are on my skin, pricking everywhere, and … like my throat is getting the air slapped out of it, and like my blood has stopped flowing through my body and is just sitting there in my veins afraid to move."

The last part, about the blood, gave her a creepy, frightened feeling. "But it was a very clever description," she said. "Maybe I'll write it down when I finish all this sliding."

"Monkey?" she called again. "Where are you?"

Still no answer.

"I'm cccccold, Monkey," she said. "Colder than I've ever been." And then, just to try out her new description, she added, "So cold that my blood has gone still in my veins."

But, ironically, now that Annalise had given so much attention to her coldness, it wasn't bothering her as much anymore, almost as if the discomfort had become more of a thought than a feeling.

"After all," she said, "it's not like I'm literally freezing. I'm just *very* uncomfortable. And this tunnel can't go on forever."

In actuality, though, she had started to wonder, if, in fact, the tunnel *could* go on forever. She had been sliding for so long, it seemed, that she could hardly even think of what it felt like to not be sliding.

"Hello down there," she called out.

"Hello, hello, hello," her own voice called back, as if mocking her attempt to make contact.

"Maybe I should start counting in my head," she thought. Singing aloud really wasn't an option because of the echo, unless, of course, she wanted to sing rounds with herself, which she did not.

"One one-thousand, two one-thousand, three one-thousand,"

she began.

"This isn't nearly as much fun as singing, but I'm going to keep on counting anyway," she said. "Four one-thousand, five one-thousand. I wonder where I am and where I'm going. Six one-thousand, seven one-thousand, eight one-thousand. And why is it so dark in here? Nine one-thousand, ten one-thousand, elev—"

But before she got to twelve, or even finished eleven, she noticed something other than blur in her field of vision. For there were shadows now, shadows of all different shapes and sizes. Some of them passed by the outside of the tunnel, and others circled around it, lingering.

"But what is that sound?" Annalise wondered, noticing that a gentle sloshing had developed around the tunnel. "There's something out there, something alive. And I'm going to find out what it is!"

She squinted her eyes a bit as they continued to adjust, and what had transformed first from blur into shadow now transformed from shadow into substance. Annalise caught, from the corner of her eye, the edge of an orange fin slipping by.

"Fish!" she squealed, with delight.

"Fish . . . fish . . . fish . . ." the tunnel called back to her, and she held her hands clasped together as she looked around to see whatever she could after having been deprived of vision in the dark tunnel for so long.

The first thing she saw clearly was a school of orange and white striped fish. Hurtling so quickly downward, she had difficulty making out details at first, but it appeared to her that the fish were dancing in pairs. A spotlight—which explained her sudden ability to see—shone on them, bouncing to and fro in time with their motions.

"It's like a big party down here," she said. "A party for fish."

She could hear chattering, laughing, and the commotion of party sounds, but all of it in a language not familiar, not *human*. It was instead a gurgling, watery language, the ancient language of the sea.

Next she saw green fish with delicate yellow flecks and thin, papery fins. They wore headlamps, like miners, and they raced downward with Annalise, waving their fins at her and smiling. A large fish used its fin to point Annalise out to a smaller one, upon which the smaller one flapped its fins with glee and bobbed up and down. Annalise began to wave back, but the green and yellow fish disappeared above her, no longer able to keep pace with her fast, downward sliding.

In the distance, Annalise could see dolphins and eels and magnificent hot pink and red coral, and closer to the tunnel there were sea horses and star fish. A brightly lit café glimmered from a remote nook in the coral, its terrace covered with fish of every imaginable shape and size. Over the café door hung an elaborate sign which looked like it was written in a kind of oceanic hieroglyphics. It depicted four of the orange and white striped fish eating sea vegetables at a table fashioned of shells. This last detail she barely caught before the café flashed out of sight.

Next she saw a group of fish kneeling in rows before an altar of some sort, which is to say that even though fish don't actually have knees, they were bent in such a way as to imply kneeling. Their fins were pressed together in front of their bodies like hands in prayer, and their heads, though not blessed with the flexibility for full bowing, were ever so slightly tipped forward. One of these fish swam up and performed a sort of ritualistic dance for the others which included lots of figure eight motions and a graceful side to side bending of the whole body. It was then that Annalise noticed the spectacular beauty of these fish, which were long and slender and aqua blue with lavender swirls and silver faces. They had lavish, flamboyant tail fins, and the one who was dancing used his as an accessory to accentuate the beauty of his dance in the same way a flamenco dancer might swish and flutter the ruffles of her dress.

But then the fish passed quickly out of sight as Annalise continued her descent through the tunnel, and as that mighty spectacle of color and beauty disappeared from view, she was left only with the fading sound of their chanting, an incantation of sorts, which was lovely and haunting and reverent.

"They certainly take their praying very seriously," Annalise thought. "I don't know what their religion is, but many blessings to them anyway."

As she continued to fall, she saw fish after fish, scene after scene, dolphin after dolphin, creature after creature. She discovered that there were many more facets of sea life than she had ever imagined, plants *and* creatures, both beautiful and homely, familiar and exotic.

The lower she went, the stranger the creatures became, some of them even emitting light. That was called bioluminescence. Annalise remembered reading about it in a book on creatures of the sea.

One fish she saw was translucent but lit from within, making it appear to be nothing but a skeleton. Another was all black except for phosphorescent yellow eyes and huge glowing jaws with hundreds of tiny sharp teeth. Annalise also saw a glowing pink weed that waved to and fro with the ocean's undulations.

The very strangest of these creatures did not resemble fish at all. One of them looked like a white elephant with flapping pink ears and pink slits for eyes. It had things that looked like legs and feet sticking out of the oddest places on its body.

"Why, I'm just in a big tunnel aquarium," Annalise said. "Only the aquarium is around me, not in front of me, and no matter which way I turn or how far down I slide, there it is, more aquarium. In fact, I am in the middle of their world, almost as if they were viewing me instead of me viewing them."

Right then a large fish swam up to the tunnel and pressed close to get a better view of Annalise. It was trying to communicate, smiling and flailing its fins about as it did, and Annalise noticed that it could swim as fast as she was falling, with seemingly little effort.

She waved.

The fish pointed downward with one of its fins, and Annalise nodded to indicate that she was aware that she was falling. The fish shook its head and pointed downward again.

Annalise's brows pulled together.

"What on earth—or under the sea—could this fish be trying to tell me?"

The fish remained in front of her and continued to point downward.

"Oh, now I get it," Annalise said. "The fish wants me to look down. I couldn't see the forest for the trees. Or, rather, I didn't see the ocean for the coral. Ha ha ha."

Annalise laughed so hard she began to shake and slap her leg.

The fish looked concerned and tried to press up closer to the glass.

I wish this fish could understand my hilarious joke, she thought. And she began to smile and nod to show the concerned fish that she was okay.

Now the fish became more frantic in its downward pointing, and Annalise realized that all the falling had made her lightheaded and had interfered with her ability to think clearly. Just how long had the fish been trying to get her to look down? She didn't know, but it was time to end the poor thing's suffering, so she turned her attention to what lay beneath the tunnel and finally understood, just in time, what the fish had been so desperate to convey.

CHAPTER SIXTEEN

SUNKEN CITY

Directly beneath Annalise, a beautiful, luminescent complex of domes sprawled across the ocean floor. In the center, the largest dome shimmered like a gargantuan violet-colored crystal. Around it, a spray of smaller domes of alternating violet and yellow hues were connected by tunnels and extended out like spokes on a wagon wheel. The tips of these spokes were connected by another series of tunnels that formed a circle around the central dome. Overlapping this circle was yet another series of small domes and tunnels that formed a square.

Annalise noticed that a spiral pattern was etched into the tops of the domes and that dead center on the central dome, the word "Yehidah" had been spelled with seashells. The dot on the "i" in "Yehidah" was a large circle through which the tunnel projected.

"Why, it's just like a huge, phosphorescent connect the dot game," Annalise said, using another term she'd learned from the book on sea creatures. "Or it's like a bull's eye. And I'm headed straight for the center of it."

She looked back up and indicated to the concerned fish that she understood she was headed for the crystal domes. The fish smiled and formed his fin into a thumbs up gesture. She gave the fish a double thumbs up. She wasn't scared. After all, this chute was just another in a series of the many passageways she'd taken since her journey had begun. She'd hopped garden stones, islands, mountaintops and clouds; she'd traversed labyrinths, garden trails, hallways and corridors; she'd gone up stairs and elevators and down tunnels, and through portals and doorways and elaborate gates.

What's more, this dome complex was just another in a series of unusual destinations. She'd been to an island that grew instruments and to magical falls; she'd been to a desert Pueblo and a garden with the book of her life; she'd even been with Mabel and Mimi to sheep heaven, and how many humans, she wondered, got to do *that*?

Chutes, domes, piece of cake, Annalise thought. I sure do miss my sheep, though. And then she thought of making up a song in their honor.

"I could sing it inside my head to avoid the echo," she said. "Or, better yet, I could use the echo as a backup singer."

But Annalise didn't have time to make up a song. She had reached the top of the central dome and was about to slide through. It looked like a long fall from the ceiling to the floor.

I sure do hope it's a soft landing, she thought.

She passed through the ceiling of the dome, and all of a sudden she stopped falling and began to float like an astronaut inside a spaceship.

"You control the pace," someone called from below. "Our minds determine almost everything here. Just imagine a safe landing, and that's what you'll get."

Annalise looked down and saw a girl about her own age holding a Persian cat. The girl lifted one of the cat's fluffy, silver, six-toed paws and waved it at Annalise.

"Rowboat says 'hello'" she called.

"Rowboat?"

"My cat. When I first got her I dreamt of being chosen to go to the surface, so I named her Rowboat. Watch this."

The girl set the cat on the ground, and it rolled onto its back and used its four legs like oars, imitating a rowing motion.

Annalise floated down as the girl had recommended and landed firmly on her feet next to Rowboat.

"Well, hello, Rowboat," she said. "You certainly are very pretty. I'm Annalise—from the Verdant Hills."

"And I am Mallory," the girl said. "Your Greeter."

It had been so long since Annalise had seen anyone her own age that she was delighted to meet Mallory. She saw her inner light extend out to Mallory in greeting, and then she saw Mallory's light meet hers and connect between them.

"I see you've found your light," Mallory said. "That's good. It will make things easier to explain."

"Indeed it will," said Rowboat.

"Oh, you talk," Annalise said to Rowboat.

She didn't know why she was surprised. Maybe because Mallory had introduced Rowboat instead of the cat introducing herself? And maybe, just possibly, Annalise still had some of the old way of thinking about her, some remnants of belief in those Earth-based rules that said cats don't talk, sheep don't sing, pigs don't fly, and cows don't jump over the moon.

"Of course I talk," Rowboat said. "One-hundred and twenty-seven languages. But it's all a bit antiquated. I prefer other methods of communication." And with that, she began to purr. "A purr conveys just about everything, I find."

Rowboat nuzzled up to Annalise's leg, rubbing her head and neck against Annalise's ankles.

"This communicates the rest," Rowboat said.

Annalise leaned over to pet Rowboat and then looked up at Mallory. "I've always loved cats," she said.

"Okay, okay," Mallory broke in. "We've all got warm fuzzies now. Let's move on before I puke."

"A true sentimentalist," Rowboat said to Annalise, with another rub on her leg. "Who else would name a cat Rowboat?"

"Please, I was five," Mallory replied. "Now I am a Greeter."

Annalise could tell there was affection in their banter, that this good-humored bickering was just one of the many games they played.

"Follow me, please," Mallory said, now turning to Annalise with a terse smile that revealed her desire to be taken seriously as a Greeter. "And I will show you around our beautiful city."

"Why, thank you," Annalise replied. "I would love that."

"Great, then we might as well start right where we are." Mallory swept her arm through the air to indicate the dome in which Annalise had landed.

"This dome," she said, "is our central and largest dome. It's the heart of our society. People come here to talk, plan, eat, celebrate. As you can see, it's divided into many, many sections. The central section is the chute, where visitors arrive."

Annalise looked around and saw that indeed the dome was divided into many sections. People sat talking in clusters on benches, and others picnicked on grassy spots. One man sat on the ledge of a fountain and sang while a small audience stood by.

"It looks like a huge park," Annalise said as she noted the activity taking place around her. There was something about the people that made her feel safe and relaxed. Their groups were different from the ones on Acoustic Island. She felt a harmony between them as they chatted among themselves and drifted peacefully from one group to another. No one was too loud or aggressive, and each group projected only the softest, most beautiful rays of light to the other groups.

The light from each group, she noticed, had a design that shifted slightly as people left or joined. This reminded her of a coloring book her mother had given her full of designs called mandalas. Each mandala was a big circle or square with smaller designs within. The book explained that the designs mean something, in the same way that words mean something, but that this meaning is understood by a deeper part of our minds than the part that understands words. The book explained that we might understand mandalas without really knowing that we understood them.

Annalise wasn't sure whether she understood them or not, but she knew that when she looked at them, she had the same feeling she got when she watched clouds drift by. It was a peaceful feeling, like she could look all day, and it wouldn't be a waste of time.

When Annalise really thought about it, she realized that, from a distance, the whole dome complex resembled a giant mandala. At any rate, the entire place was peaceful, all except for the monkey, who Annalise could now see bouncing from group to group, like some kind of deranged maniac, leaving a trail of grimy energy behind him. It smeared itself over the designs of the groups like a charcoal smudge on a pastel drawing. The people in the groups simply said "hello" to Monkey as he passed by and then continued about their activities as if the smudge had never happened. Eventually the smudge disappeared.

"The light is more prominent here than anywhere else I've been," Annalise said to Mallory and Rowboat. "I can even see designs. Boy, is that crazy monkey making a mess!"

"Actually," Mallory said, "I'm glad you brought that up. Do you think you could control your monkey?"

"Me control the monkey?"

"Well, I don't mean to be rude or anything, but you can see how much trouble he's causing," Mallory replied.

"Indeed," said Rowboat, whose nose was all scrunched up in an expression of disgust. "That is one ruckus loving beast."

"Well, okay, let me see what I can do," Annalise said, and she set out after Monkey.

Let's see, Annalise thought. When Monkey was small, I could keep him in my pocket where he wouldn't bother anyone, so the trick is probably to try to get him small and manageable again. Also, when he's small, he's sometimes an inanimate key instead of a hyper monkey.

She turned back to Mallory and Rowboat.

"Do you have any food?" she asked.

"Sure," Mallory replied. "We'll have lunch at the dining hall."

"It's not for me. I meant is there any food I can use to catch the monkey?"

"Does your monkey like bananas?" Mallory asked.

"He does, but he can be quite mischievous with the peels," Annalise replied, giggling just a little bit from the memory of Hagski's expression when Monkey went down the chute.

"Oh, dear. Oh, dear. I certainly don't mean to intrude," Rowboat said. "But won't feeding the monkey give it more energy and help it to grow, when what we really want is for it to be smaller, calmer and tamer?"

"Why, yes. That's true," Annalise said. "But how can I catch it besides with food?"

"Well," Rowboat said. "It seems to me that if it's *your* monkey, which it certainly is, then you only have to command it, and it must do as you say. There's no need to catch it at all. In fact, I'm not really clear on how it got so far away from you in the first place."

"Honestly," Annalise said, "I didn't even know I had it until this sweet old lady at the pueblo gave me a key. But now I'm just embarrassed and frustrated with it most of the time. I kind of wish I could go back to not even knowing I had it."

"Oh, don't you worry," Rowboat said, patting Annalise on the leg with her paw. "Ignorance is never best. That wise old woman did you a favor by helping you discover your monkey. Don't be embarrassed about him. Most of the visitors who come here have them. That's why the people in the park are so good at ignoring their antics."

"But this *is* a good place to learn to control your monkey," Mallory added. "That's why the old woman gave you the key. If you can tame your monkey, then you'll be much better off than if you had never known you had one."

"That would be great," Annalise said. "But how do I do it? He's never listened to a thing I've said."

"Be polite but firm," Rowboat said.

"It's the only way," Mallory agreed.

"Okay, wish me luck."

With that, Annalise was off to discipline her monkey.

CHAPTER SEVENTEEN

BODHISATTVA

Annalise found that Mallory and Rowboat were quite right. She had only to walk up to Monkey and firmly command him, and he was back in her pocket where he belonged. She was pleased to have control of him so quickly, especially since, just moments before, she hadn't known it was possible. But there was also something nagging at her. Just exactly what was her relationship to Monkey, anyway? Mallory and Rowboat seemed to see Monkey's behavior as Annalise's responsibility and even a reflection on Annalise herself.

As she walked back over to Mallory and Rowboat, she noticed that the ceiling looked like a beautiful blue sky with big fluffy clouds.

"But that's not what I want you to see right now," Mallory said. "Look past the sky, at the ceiling itself." And suddenly Annalise could see past the clouds to the structure behind them.

"Our domes and tunnels are constructed of pure amethyst and adhere to the golden ratio."

"The golden ratio?" Annalise said.

"Everything is proportioned according to the mathematical constant of approximately 1.6180339887."

"That's what you call 'approximate?'"

Mallory and Rowboat laughed.

"But what in the world does that mean?" Annalise asked.

"It's when two things that are put together have sizes that match a specific formula. For example, let's say you have a dog, and that dog is a certain size."

"Okay." Annalise nodded.

"And then you have a puppy, and that puppy is a certain size."

"Got it."

"Well, the dog is a certain amount bigger than the puppy, right?"

Annalise nodded.

"And if you put the puppy and the dog together, they are bigger than the dog alone, right?"

"Right."

"So if you look at how much bigger the dog is than the puppy and then how much bigger the combination is than the dog alone, and you see that these two amounts are the same, you have a golden ratio."

"Yes, I get it," Annalise said.

"Clever girl, this one," Rowboat said.

"Yep," Mallory replied. "So anyway, I'm sure you noticed from outside that we've squared the circle with our smaller domes and tunnels and that seven is a prominent number in our groupings. There are seven spokes, seven domes per spoke, seven tunnels between domes, and so forth. We use the ratio with our artwork, too."

She swept her hand to indicate a group of paintings on the wall. They were of many different subjects. One was a single sea shell with rays of light coming from it, and another was of a school of fish swimming inside a rose bud. Others were abstract or non-representational, like the mandalas from Annalise's coloring book, but all of the paintings had the same feel to them, the same peaceful mood, and Annalise could sense this peace in her body, like a warm humming.

"1.6180339887, all of it."

"It's amazing," Annalise said. "So beautiful. I know this sounds crazy, but I think I can feel it humming."

"That's sacred geometry for you. Once it was misinterpreted as perfection, but we understand it now as a spark of the divine. Everything is a tiny model of the whole of all things. We have a greeting here that goes, 'I honor the place in you where the whole universe lives. I honor the place in you that is love, truth, and peace. When you are in that place in you, and I am in that place in me, we are one.' We call that greeting 'namaste' for short, and we call the hum you mentioned 'om.'"

"Amazing," Annalise said once again. "I've heard my mom use those words before, but I didn't really understand what they meant, not like this."

"Your mom was teaching you gradually," Mallory said. "In the Earth way. Things are faster here."

They walked to the dining hall, and Mallory continued her explanation of each of the domes they passed through. There were art domes, reading domes, music domes, philosophy domes, mathematics domes, science domes, dancing domes, martial arts domes, and so on. Every room seemed devoted to some form of art, study, or physical recreation, and Annalise could see that all of the activities were performed in the spirit of playfulness and joy. These people took such delight in their activities that it seemed silly to even think of the activities as work.

"How are people assigned to their specific tasks?" Annalise asked.

Rowboat giggled.

"Nobody assigns them," Mallory said. "People just do what they want."

"Then how does everything get done?" Annalise asked.

"There's nothing that actually *needs* to be done," Mallory said. "Any 'progress' that's made happens because people hit upon it while doing what they love. That's the inventive spirit within us all."

"But how does that work?"

"It's not about work," Mallory replied. "It's about contribution and harmony. When we sense our connection, we know what to do."

"So when you said you were a greeter now, you literally meant *right now*. You might do something else tomorrow?"

"Correct."

"And what about going to the surface? You mentioned having to be chosen for that."

"Ah, yes. Well, that's different because it involves leaving our community. It's a great honor and also a great sacrifice to be chosen. There are many people each year who petition for permission to go to the surface, but most are not allowed. The entire community must agree unanimously in order for permission to be granted to a single person. It's a very rare and special occurrence."

"What do they do when they get there?"

"Live among the people."

"That's it?" Annalise asked, disappointed. "There must be more."

"There's more." Mallory said. "The idea is to help humanity evolve as we did. We want to help, but we learned early on that we have to go slowly and not scare people off. When we weren't careful before, we were called lunatics, heretics, sorcerers, witches. It can be quite dangerous if we're not careful."

"How awful."

"Don't worry. We know what to do now. We go as artists and scientists. It may not always be pleasant up there, but we've learned to manage with fewer and fewer problems. In art, we can present our truths as fantasies without having them questioned. It allows us to share our ideas. This paves the way for science to make 'discoveries' later on. One way you can recognize us up there is that our talents are varied, just as they are here. You might use the term 'Renaissance.'"

"You mean like Leonardo Da Vinci? Wow. And you would give up this wonderful life to go up and help like that?"

"Without question," Mallory replied.

"And Rowboat?"

"It's complicated. Let's eat, and I'll explain everything."

They entered the dining hall, which had the appearance of a lovely outdoor café. Vines threaded their way through fences, awnings hung overhead, and tiny white bulbs, like Christmas lights, shimmered from the trees.

"What would you eat if you could have anything you wanted right now?" Rowboat asked.

"Well, that's not possible," Annalise said, "because it would be my mom's spaghetti, and only my mom knows how to make that."

Mallory winked at Rowboat.

"Mom's spaghetti please," Rowboat said, and a plate appeared in front of Annalise. Sure enough, the signature green Spanish olives with their little red centers lay nestled among mounds of noodles and chunky red sauce.

"Actually, make it two," Rowboat said. "That looks great."

Mallory held up three fingers.

"Three," Rowboat said. "And three waters, please."

"Wow," Annalise said. "I could almost pretend my mom's just around the corner."

"You'll see your mom soon enough," Mallory said.

"How soon?" Annalise scooted to the edge of her seat.

"Soon, if you want. I promise. I know it's hard, but try to concentrate on what I'm about to say. It's important."

Annalise nodded and set down her fork.

"Your question about Rowboat. You were worried that I would leave my pet behind."

Again, Annalise nodded, wide-eyed.

"Things aren't exactly as they appear here. You noticed the light is stronger here, right?"

"Yes."

"That's because we've evolved beyond our necessity for physical form. These forms you see us in right now, we take them off and put them on the way you change clothes. So a cat, for instance—"

"Isn't really a cat?"

"Correct. It's just another one of us taking form."

"And the names?"

"The same. We have other means by which to recognize each other."

"So when you said you'd named Rowboat, you just meant for while Rowboat takes this form. You were joking about having named her when you were five?"

"Sort of. Rowboat and I incarnated to greet you. We took forms we thought would be pleasing to you. We acted in a way that felt natural to our forms, to make you feel comfortable."

"Well, it certainly worked!" Annalise said. "I like both of you very much. But—"

"Yes?"

"Can I see how you really look?"

"Anytime," Rowboat replied. "You can see energy, right?"

Annalise nodded. She thought about how at the park the groups not only had patterns of color and light, but the individuals did, too.

"If you look carefully, each of us has a distinct marking at the center of our pattern, sort of like a watermark on the page of a book."

Annalise saw that it was true. She could see their energy if she just looked at it, like when she looked beyond the clouds and blue sky to the true structure of the amethyst ceiling. She could see that many of the energy beings who had not taken physical form were in the café, right there with them.

"How often do you take form?" Annalise asked.

"There's no regularity to it," Rowboat replied. "Sometimes we want to have experiences through form, but we're always content in our light bodies. It could be months or even years between incarnations, or in some phases we may incarnate every 'day.' We don't really experience time the same way you do."

"What makes you decide to take form?"

"We do it when we think we have something to contribute. It's not something we necessarily *like* to do. There's pleasure in taking form, but there can be a lot of pain, too."

"Are you Buddhists?"

Rowboat chuckled.

"No," Mallory said. "Why?"

"My mom reads me books about all different religions, and there is one book I really like called *Bodhisattva*. It has these people who agree to not accept total peace until all other living beings have also found peace. It's a sacrifice, just like when you go to the surface."

"Well, that's lovely," Rowboat said. "But there's no need to label what we do."

"That's right," Mallory said. "When we started our lives as humans on the surface, long ago, we were all different religions, but we were a primitive manifestation of those religions, full of hatred for anything that was different from ourselves. After lifetimes of violence, we learned to respect each others' beliefs, and, as our tolerance grew, we eventually found that our belief systems weren't necessary at all, so we took them off, just like we take off our forms. We became as we are now, pure energy, with nothing between us and the divine. That's why we prefer not to label or be labeled."

"That's a lot to think about," Annalise said.

"That's why I wanted us to sit down and take this slowly," Mallory said. "It's important to understand about tolerance, especially religious tolerance. It's the only way."

"What she's saying is that all religions have similarities and that these are the real truths. The differences among them, those things that people fight over, are not the deeper truths," Rowboat said.

"Right," Mallory said. "Take the golden rule, for instance: Do unto others as you would have them do unto you. This exists in some form in all major religions, and if we all did that, there would be no war or violence."

"But why are you telling me this? I'm just one of them."

"No, Annalise," Rowboat said. "There is no them and us. That's the point. You know these things when you're born into your bodies, but you forget them as you grow. You're so caught up in your human lives, in that exciting illusion, that you forget who and what you really are. You need to understand this if you are to help."

"Help?"

"You must know that's why you came here, to remember the things you knew before you were born and to prepare to go back and work among those of us on the surface."

"But I don't know how to do that," Annalise said. "I'm just a little girl. I want to go home."

"No Annalise. You're not a little girl. You're a very old soul, and you *are* home. You're always home when you're processing understanding. The pull to your Earth life is strong. You've made deep connections, but you're at a crossroads. Your body, your human form, is in that hospital bed. You can leave it forever. You have accumulated enough merit in your many, well-lived lifetimes to join us in this peaceful existence. Or you can decide to go back and do our work. You are one of the special few who would be granted memory of all of this for the remainder of your lifetime should you choose to go back. It will be a sacrifice, but it will be so very worth it. The third and final option, of course, is to go back with no memory of any of this and live out a normal human life."

"I don't know," Annalise said, pouting a little. "I wouldn't know how to do it."

"Your music," Rowboat said.

"What?"

"You'll know exactly what to do," Mallory said. "Why do you think we put you through all those tests: harmonizing the musicians, finding your mother, taming the monkey, guiding your sheep to the right pasture? We had to make sure."

"Is this what all of your 'visitors' come here for?"

"Yes. Those who are able to do our work are given a choice, and it must be their own decision. You were dead for a brief while, and now your human body is in a coma while you decide."

Annalise was quiet for a minute as she thought about that body back in the hospital room.

"So if I decide to go back and help, that's it. I'll be on the surface with my mom again, back in my old body?"

"Yes, but it's not quite that simple. You can't do it for the wrong reasons. You must do it for humanity, or your Annalise body will die, and you'll be reborn into a new body with no memory of this. If you only want to go back to your old life, then it's better to return without memories."

"And if I say I don't want to go back?"

"Then everything you've accomplished here will be rewarded. As I said, you've already accumulated enough merit to stay here if you want."

"But what *is* here? Is this Heaven?"

Rowboat smiled and patted the top of Annalise's hand.

"Such a need to label things," she said.

"No, this is not Heaven," Mallory replied. "But it is very close. Eventually we will all move on, but as I said, not until *everyone* moves on."

Annalise thought of those many evenings at home, snuggled up beside her mother on the couch, looking at illustrations while her mother read *Bodhisattva* aloud. She thought of her favorite part, when the character makes the choice to postpone her own enlightenment for the sake of others, and how she asked her mother to read that same page over and over. She was fascinated by the picture of a woman holding up a whole palmful of miniature people to a radiant light. She looked so happy when she did that.

"Your mother is special," Mallory said, looking deep into Annalise's eyes. "You chose her for a reason."

Something suddenly dawned on Annalise as she began to comprehend Mallory's words.

"I've been preparing for this all along, haven't I?" she said.

Mallory and Rowboat smiled at each other and at Annalise. Annalise felt the hum.

"I'll do it," she said.

"Yes, yes, of course you will," Rowboat said.

"I never doubted it," Mallory said.

Annalise started to say something back, but just as she began to speak, she felt suddenly lighter, almost like she was floating. And then, from the top of her head, something fluttered, something beautiful.

"Oh, my gosh," Annalise said. "My silver cord. It was there all along, right in the one place I would never look, the top of my own head."

She turned to see if Mallory and Rowboat had heard her, but all she saw were lights—two glorious, beautiful lights. She saw that they were Rowboat and Mallory, back in their true forms.

They pulsed at her, and she pulsed back.

CHAPTER EIGHTEEN

PIT STOP

Annalise grabbed hold of the silver cord that extended from the top of her head and pulled herself up by it just as if she were climbing a rope in gym class. Hand over hand. One move at a time. Since the rope was connected to her head, the higher she got, the more slack there was in the part of the rope between her hands and her head. It draped beneath her in a huge and ever-growing loop.

Annalise had no idea, once again, where she was or where she was headed.

Then she chuckled over the word "headed."

"Literally," she thought. "I am literally *headed* somewhere. Gosh, I'm so funny. And I remind myself of someone right now, too. Who could it be?"

She scratched her head with one hand while grasping the rope with the other.

"Oh, yes. Tony and his crazy humor. It must have rubbed off on me!"

Annalise looked around, and all she could see was sky.

"I'm not in the dome anymore, that's certain," she said. "Nor the ocean."

She continued to hoist, hand over hand, steadily, easily, until she saw something in the distance up above, something white and fluffy.

"Clouds. Oh, goodness," she said to herself. "I thought I was done with all that."

Then, as if on cue, she heard Hagski's screeching voice yell out, "Well, if it isn't good ole'Jack, come up his pathetic, mite infested beanstalk to see the grumpy giant. Fee Fie Foe Fum. Is that what you want to hear? Yada yada yada. Blah blah blah. What do you want this time? My harp? My golden eggs? A bag of coins? Forget it. You'll get nothing from me, Missy. You hear that? Nothing."

Annalise could feel Monkey beginning, like a lone jumping bean, to bounce around in her pocket at the sound of Hagski's voice.

"Well, if it isn't Little Miss Monkey. I know you found him. I can see him in your pocket. Give him back, thief."

Annalise, who had just pulled herself through the clouds, began to look around. Hagski, she saw, stood in a dramatic posture of indignation: hands on hips, jaw jutted out, back arched, lips pursed. Her hair was wild as ever, sticking out this way and that, in large clumps, just as if she'd stuck her finger in a light socket. Now, in addition to the pink streaks, there were also purple streaks, orange streaks, and banana yellow streaks protruding erratically in no discernible pattern.

"No," Annalise said. "I'm keeping the monkey."

Hagski tapped her foot.

"Well, if you're going to be belligerent and refuse to hand over *my* monkey, you might as well tell me what you want. So what is it? What do you want?"

She huffed and puffed.

I guess I'd be angry, too, if I had Hagski's hairdresser, Annalise thought. Or her wardrobist.

Hagski was wearing one of the most hideous get-ups Annalise had ever seen: a bright purple T-shirt with a yellow flower in the middle of the chest, orange baggy pants with black skulls and crossbones all over them, aqua blue toe socks, and clunky brown suede sandals. Over the socks, hanging just above the left sandal top, was a delicate silver anklet with a heart charm.

"Well, I'm not quite sure what I want. Honestly, I didn't even mean to come here."

"No one ever does," Hagski replied. "But you *do want* something. That's how you end up here. So what is it? What else do you want, monkey thief?"

Just then, Annalise noticed something in Hagski's demeanor that she hadn't noticed before: although she projected an air of confrontational indignation, there was a certain vulnerability underneath this facade. Annalise noticed for the first time how childlike Hagski's actual features were. Her nose was small and delicate and ever so slightly turned up at the tip, and her big, round eyes were as green as spring's first blades of grass. Her cheeks and jaw had about them the particular curves and rosy blush of a doll's face, and her lips were a perfect little pout.

"Why, you're not as mean as all that," Annalise said. "I can see right through you. And you can't do a thing to me. You have no real power over me."

"Why you little—you little—you—"

Before Hagski could get the words out, her body began to convulse and spasm in a fit of seizures. Her head jerked to and fro, flipping her outlandish hair this way and that in blur of color.

Seeing that her words were doing the trick, Annalise continued.

"I know you can't do a thing to me. You're weak, a parasite. I saw that you had no energy and had to take mine. I saw it when you tried to take the key from me before, and I see it now, too."

Hagski's body continued to convulse.

"You can't do anything without me," Annalise said. "I don't need you; it's you who needs me."

With this last statement, Hagski's body made one huge, final convulsion, and a ghostly form shot from her body and into the space between her and Annalise, where it wavered like a mirage.

The shell of Hagski's former body crumpled in on itself, dissolved into dust and blew away.

"I guess the pen *is* mightier than the sword," Annalise said.

She started to congratulate herself once again on her clever wit, but before she could say anything about it, she felt herself being drawn quickly toward the ghostly Hagski, as if someone had turned an enormous vacuum cleaner toward her. She tried to resist the pull, but her strength in no way matched the powerful force drawing her toward Hagski. She made a feeble, nearly indiscernible, jerk backwards. And then, SMACK. Before she could do anything about it, they were merged. Annalise and Hagski. Hagski and Annalise. Together as one.

"Gross!" Annalise yelled. "I'm stuck to Hagski. Help! Somebody help me."

She shook her leg, as if Hagski might come pouring out of her foot if she shook hard enough. When that didn't work, she began patting herself forcefully on the chest, while coughing at the same time, as loudly as she could. No Hagski.

Annalise began running in circles, and then started jumping up and down and looking beneath her feet to see where Hagski had gone.

"Why, this is ridiculous," she said. "I must look as silly as a dog chasing its tail. I had better stop all this nonsense." And then she sat down to instead think about what had happened.

"Well, I don't really feel different," she said. "You'd think I would feel terrible to suddenly have a Hagski in me."

She held her arm up and examined it. Same arm. Then she fanned her hair out in front of her face. No purple streaks.

"I still look like me," she said. "And I still feel like me. In fact, nothing is really different at all."

Something suddenly dawned on Annalise, and she slapped her hand to her forehead. "Oh, my gosh. That's it," she said. "Nothing is different at all. I've always had a Hagski in me, just like I've always had Monkey in me and didn't know it. Hagski and Monkey were just me all along, getting in my own way."

Annalise heard a different voice now, a nice one.

"Those voices that get in your way and tell you what you can't do are dependent on your cooperation. If you know this, they lose their power."

It was Bob. Annalise jumped up and hugged him.

"I'm not saying they won't ever come back, just that *you* can tell *them* what to do now. You're done," he said, smiling.

"You mean I get to go back home?" she asked, pulling away from the hug to look at Bob as she spoke to him.

"Yes, but there's something I want you to remember," Bob said.

"Sure," Annalise replied. "What is it?"

"Just remember," Bob said. "*Always* remember, that the most beautiful and authentic worlds are inside your very own self, and you can always find them."

Annalise nodded, wide-eyed.

"Remember also, Annalise, that these worlds exist inside all living beings and in every part of the fabric of this life. So when you meet another person, no matter how small or insignificant they may seem to you, and no matter how big their monkeys or how loud their Hagskis, always be sure to honor the majestic depths that reside beneath their skin, even if they, themselves, are not aware of these depths. Do you understand?"

"I do," Annalise replied.

"And treat everything with respect. Everything."

Annalise nodded.

"Good. All that's left now is to follow the silver cord."

"But I did follow the silver cord, and it led me here," Annalise said.

"Ah, that was nothing," Bob said. "Just a pit stop."

"Will I be seeing you anymore?"

"Not so much, but I'll always be around, like an old tree in the background, if you really need me."

"Bob?"

"Yes?"

"I," Annalise faltered a bit. "Um—I love you."

"I love you, too, Annalise. Very much."

Annalise smiled.

"And one last thing," Bob said.

"What's that?"

"Please tell your mother I love her, too."

"My mother?"

And then, in a flash, Bob was gone, leaving behind a brilliant trail of light that flickered above Annalise's head.

CHAPTER NINETEEN

WAKING

When Annalise woke up, she was indeed in the hospital bed, just as she'd expected, buried beneath a pile of covers and hooked up to various cords and machines. The machines hummed and blinked dots of light in patterns that looked to Annalise like fairies skipping across the top of a river. She longed to chase after them, just as she had done the day she got caught in the flood.

"But that was no fairy," she said. "That was Bob."

She then turned her attention to the wall in front of her bed and noticed, hanging there, the painting she loved so much, the one of the outdoor flower market. As she looked at it, she vaguely remembered that sometime not long ago she'd followed a bright yellow light that illuminated a silver cord. She liked that cord better than the dull, gray, electrical cords she saw now.

"That was Bob, too. My guide. He wasn't really gone. He led me back here through the tunnel."

She looked to her left and saw her mom—her real, true mom—sleeping beside her as if she'd been there all along, feet propped up on the recliner, just waiting for what she knew in her infinite faith would eventually happen: that her daughter would wake up.

Beside her was a stand with a radio set to the classical station. From its speakers softly emanated a whimsical Tchaikovsky piece that Annalise recognized but couldn't name.

"Mom," Annalise thought. "Mom, I'm back. I decided to come back, and I have the memories. I know what to do." But when she actually opened her mouth to speak, all that came out was a feeble, "Mom."

Annalise's mom began to stir, and she murmured something only half intelligible, some question as to whether she herself were dreaming or awake.

"Awake, Mom," Annalise said. "We're awake."

Annalise's mom rubbed her eyes, blinked a few times, and then stared in disbelief for about a split second before throwing her feet quickly over the side of the recliner.

Soon she stood beside Annalise, speechless, tears streaming down her face. For an instant, she stared at Annalise in wonder, smiling at her through her tears and rubbing her cheek with the palm of her hand. Then, quickly, with the other hand, she pushed a button over Annalise's bed.

"She's awake," she said as she released the button.

Behind Annalise's mom, a door opened—the one with the handle Annalise hadn't been able to grasp on her journey over from the pueblo—and a throng of doctors and nurses rushed in, bringing with them a sudden flurry of stethoscopes and scrubs, moving feet and busy hands. They checked machines, looked into her eyes, listened to her heart and lungs. They asked her mom questions: How long had Annalise been awake? Had she said anything yet? Had she moved much?

Annalise's mom answered questions while never letting go of Annalise's hand or losing eye contact. She had already told Annalise she loved her about ten times just in the few minutes she'd been awake.

"I just can't believe it," she kept saying. And, "Somebody tell me this is real."

It was all happening so fast that to anyone looking on it would appear chaotic, but to Annalise and her mom, who had both just woken up, the rapid and intense activity had a dreamlike quality.

Annalise could, in fact, see the scene almost as if she were observing it, yet she was a participant, too. She was there, all right, really and truly there, inside her body, feeling the pulse of that human life she had decided to live after all.

She started to move her arm, but she felt a sharp pain shoot from her elbow to her wrist, and she put it back down on the bed. This physical pain, she understood, would soon enough have its end, and she knew that within herself, even at the very same moment the pain was occurring, was also the capacity to transcend it. The trick was, like with the cold in the tunnel, to accept it instead of trying to pretend it wasn't there. She instinctively knew that it would make her stronger in the long run and that it would help her to be more compassionate.

She meant to say something about this, to explain it to the doctors and her mother, but she felt a wave of drowsiness come over her, like a tide pulling her gently back beneath the ocean of sleep.

She was simultaneously in two worlds, the inner and the outer, and her mind was somehow in touch with both.

"There will be time," she heard a voice call out from the dreaming world. "There will be time." And she let go of whatever it was she meant to say, knowing that she'd have another opportunity.

Flickering and fluttering around her, the energy of the doctors, the nurses, and her mother poured into her, made her feel better. She could feel their vibrations, see their light.

"Don't try to say too much," a doctor said. "Test the waters. See how you feel."

"It's like my body's half-dead." Annalise said, and this time she made sure her words came out. "But everything else feels good."

"Everything else?" the doctor asked, raising his eyebrows.

"Yes, everything else."

The doctors and nurses looked at Annalise's mom to see if she could offer an explanation, but she just lifted her shoulders in response.

"Don't you worry, Mrs. Humphrey," one of the nurses said. "She'll be making sense soon enough."

"That's right, honey," another nurse said, patting Annalise's mom's arm.

Annalise looked outside. A happily chirping row of birds lined a tree branch near the window.

"Why, if I were a bird, I would just fly, fly, fly all day," Annalise thought.

"But we won't leave until you're better," the birds thought back. "You'll need us watching over you as long as you're stuck in that little room."

"Oh, thank you so much," Annalise thought back to the birds. "It will help me pass time if I can watch you from the window."

A nurse fiddled with Annalise's IV, and her attention was drawn back to the room.

She knew the nurses didn't have the knowledge she came back with, that if she tried to explain what she meant by "everything else," it wouldn't make sense to them. But all the same, they looked like angels to her, offering comfort to her and to her mother. She could see how the light transferred off their hands as they touched her, and she felt waves of gentle energy that she knew would help her to heal.

She thought back to when she knew so little, when she first arrived in the land of the clouds.

"I was singing a song with my sheep. What was that?" she thought. And then, "Oh, yes. I know."

"Oh, it's a Sunny Saturday, Sunny Saturday indeed," she sang weakly, aloud, and her singing cast a momentary spell over the doctors and nurses, who had never before heard of anyone coming out of a coma singing.

"But how could she?" A nurse interrupted.

"Sing at a time like this?" Annalise's mom asked. She beamed a proud smile. "You don't know my daughter!"

"Well, that, too," the nurse said. "But how on earth could she know it's Saturday when she has been in a coma for six weeks now and has only just woken up?"

"I know lots of things," Annalise replied. "Like about Mabel and Mimi, that they're in the sky pasture with Me Anyou. And the songs in my head. I need to write them down."

Annalise turned her head toward her mom, "And, Mom, did you know that every whole thing is part of something bigger even though it's also complete? We are so very, very huge, and also very, very small. And Mom, I almost forgot. My guide, Bob, he told me to tell you he loves you."

At this, Annalise's mom released Annalise's hand for the first time since she'd been awake. She took a few steps backwards and plopped into the recliner without looking back.

"Bob? Bob who?"

"I don't know, just Bob."

Everyone was shocked by Annalise's sudden burst of speech, especially after she'd had such difficulty speaking just moments before.

Annalise's mom looked to be in deep thought on the recliner, and it was as if all the activity in the room had frozen for just a minute. Everyone waited for her to speak.

"What did this 'Bob' look like, honey?" she asked.

"Well," Annalise said, "I don't know. He was awfully clever. He knew everything, and whenever I needed him he always seemed to appear out of nowhere. He looked like a regular man, I guess, except that he was made out of light."

Annalise's mom nodded.

"And his hand? Did you notice anything about either one of his hands?" she asked.

"Well, one of them had a scar shaped like a heart," Annalise said, yawning. She had begun to feel quite drowsy again, and found it harder and harder to stay awake. "Does that count?"

Annalise's mom smiled a teary smile.

"Yes, it does, sweetheart," she said.

Then Annalise started to say something else, but a nurse interrupted to say that Annalise needed to get some rest. She gave Annalise's mom a stern look that said, "Pull back on the emotion. The girl's exhausted."

"You two can talk more later," she said.

She must have noticed a worried look in Annalise's eyes, because she patted Annalise's hand softly and said, "Don't worry, honey. It's safe to rest. You'll wake up again."

"That's right," the doctor said. "You'll need less and less rest as the weeks progress."

The doctor began talking to Annalise's mom about what to expect through the recovery process, and Annalise heard her mom talking about how her body had been carried away by the rushing, rising waters, which had thrown her against tree trunks and rocks. She must have already been unconscious when this happened, because she had no recollection of it whatsoever.

She tried to stay awake, to listen more, but she couldn't help drifting off, and soon she found herself in a land that was half dream and half memory, that land of her earliest days, of the times before her father had died. In her dream she was in bed, just as she was in bed now, but it was not the hospital bed of the present. It was instead the first small bed she'd had as a child.

"Another," she said in the dream. "Please."

"Okay, but only one more," her mother replied.

Then, instead of just her mother's voice, there were two—two voices singing the refrain of her favorite lullaby to her one last time. And just as she was starting to drift off into another sleep, the sleep *inside* her dream, she saw, barely illuminated by the nightlight, a hand on the doorknob before her parents tiptoed out of the room. On the web between the thumb and index finger, there was a heart-shaped scar.

"My God," Annalise said, waking up momentarily. "Bob. Robert. *Dad*."

She tried to stand up to go to the other side of the room where her mom was talking to a doctor, but another sharp pain shot through her legs, and she allowed herself to gently fall back onto the bed.

"Now, now," one of the nurses said, pulling the covers back up. "You need to be more careful while those limbs heal up. I'm going to give you something for the pain, and you just rest. Your body's not used to all this activity right now."

And though Annalise meant to respond, she felt the waves of drowsiness overtake her again, and before she knew it, she was back in that place between waking and dreams. In the background she could still hear the voices of the doctors and nurses, their gentle murmurs ebbing and flowing in sync with the rhythms of her journey toward sleep. She tried to listen to what they said, but as she became more attuned to the cadences of their speech, the words gradually lost shape, and she felt herself slipping deeper and deeper into the world of her dream, that comfortable place, built by her own mind —

"Why, I'm still wearing my hospital gown," she said in her dream. "Even though I'm outside. But my leg doesn't hurt anymore."

She began to drift downward as she walked through the woods and toward the river at the base of the Verdant Hills. As she walked, animals gathered and followed her down the path, animals of every kind, both wild and domesticated, furred and feathered, winged and legged; and soon there were reptiles, too, slithering behind and hopping along; and insects, even butterflies and ladybugs and honeybees. And all these creatures formed a circle around Annalise that moved with her as she walked. She cooed to them and petted them, but she did not stop walking for even a minute. She just kept moving, compelled by her legs and her feet to reach the river, knowing no other thought than to get to the muddy banks.

As she got closer, she saw a huge, open clearing and, inside it, a piano and a wooden bench. The bench had a beautiful, padded red velvet cushion, and Annalise sat down at this bench and placed just the barest tips of her fingers on the cool, smooth keys of the piano. A bird, one of the group from outside her hospital window, perched on her shoulder and sang a perfect, clear note, and then Annalise began to play, gently at first, but then more vigorously as she gained confidence in her new skill.

Her eyes were closed as she played, but she could see. She could see the wisps of color rise from the keys and into the air where they curled around the corners of the evening and drifted into the sky.

More and more animals came out from behind trees, out of the river and down from the sky, even more animals than Annalise had ever known were there. And soon people started to come, too, people of all sizes, ages, and ethnicities. They were dressed in a vast array of garbs that indicated homes in both near and remote regions of the world. Some were casual, in jeans and T-shirts, and others were formal, in robes, beads, and tribal dress. These people gathered around the piano and sat along the banks of the river.

Everywhere Annalise looked there was life, on the ground and in the river, and even in the twinkling sky. And the more she played, the more they came and the more the color streamed from the piano's keys, until it was spreading everywhere, the color, curling around people and animals and wrapping itself around trees and the stems of plants. And when Annalise opened her mouth to sing, the color streamed from it, as well, twirling and looping and diving, just as with the notes themselves.

"I've never seen anything like it," said a woman in a sari as she crept in closer to get a better look.

"Nor I," said a tall man in a sombrero.

Another man boosted a small boy up onto his shoulders. "Can you see?" he asked the boy. "What is it?"

"It's a girl singing and playing the piano," the boy said.

"But the color, son. What is it? Where is it coming from?"

"It's coming from the girl," the boy said.

He reached up and touched a stream of blue that lingered above his head. As he touched it, a rush of purple coursed through the blue, and he touched that, too. Soon pink and yellow and even colors he had never seen before surged through that main strand of blue. For a moment, he was speechless while he touched them all, opening his hand so that the colors could thread between his outstretched fingers.

"It feels like love," he said.

"It does," said the woman standing next to him. "It feels like love."

The boy saw that the woman also had her hand in a colorful stream of light. He saw that her hand glowed, infused by the color.

"I want to touch it," said a girl. "Put me up, Daddy."

"Me, too," said another girl, reaching out to touch a strand that wavered directly in front of her.

Soon everyone was reaching out to touch the color, and the color connected them like the strands of a web, each to the other, body to body, mind to mind, heart to heart. They felt safe and happy and unified, and they sang. And when they sang they made their own strands of color, color that they shared with each other.

And Annalise smiled, knowing that her journey had begun.

About the Author

Melissa Studdard is a professor at Lone Star College-Tomball, a book reviewer at-large for *The National Poetry Review*, and a contributing editor for both *Tiferet* and *The Criterion*. For *Tiferet*, she hosts the radio interview program, *Tiferet Talk*. Her stories, poems, essays, reviews, and articles have appeared in dozens of magazines and journals. She currently lives in Texas with her daughter and their four cats.

For more information, please visit www.melissastuddard.com.

To play *Six Weeks to Yehidah*-related games, please go to www.sixweekstoyehidah.com.

ALL THINGS THAT MATTER PRESS ™

FOR MORE INFORMATION ON TITLES AVAILABLE FROM
ALL THINGS THAT MATTER PRESS, GO TO
http://allthingsthatmatterpress.com
or contact us at
allthingsthatmatterpress@gmail.com